# THE BORN LEADER

# THE BORN LEADER

## UNSTOPPABLE LIV BEAUFONT™ BOOK 12

### SARAH NOFFKE

### MICHAEL ANDERLE

DISRUPTIVE IMAGINATION

LMBPN Publishing
PMB 196, 2540 South Maryland Pkwy
Las Vegas, NV 89109

First US Edition, September 2019
eBook ISBN: 978-1-64202-478-4
Print ISBN: 978-1-64202-479-1

THE BORN LEADER TEAM


## Thanks to the JIT Readers

Jackey Hankard-Brodie
Nicole Emens
Deb Mader
Misty Roa
Angel LaVey
Dorothy Lloyd
Peter Manis
Kelly O'Donnell
Jeff Eaton
Larry Omans

*If I've missed anyone, please let me know!*

## Editor
The Skyhunter Editing Team

*For Trudy.*
*The first day we met, you called me a tiger.*
*Still my favorite college class ever. And the one that flamed my*
*fire for writing.*
*— Sarah*

*To Family, Friends and*
*Those Who Love*
*to Read.*
*May We All Enjoy Grace*
*to Live the Life We Are*
*Called.*
*— Michael*

# CHAPTER ONE

Terror ran down Liv Beaufont's spine like a sharp tack, needling each of her vertebrae. She tensed against the wall, trying to slow her breathing.

Never before had she felt such fear. It tore at her insides. Made her want to run as fast as her magic could take her. Hide under the covers. But there were no covers, she reminded herself. Just the darkness in this seemingly endless maze.

Liv knew the fear wasn't real, only imagined, but it was hard to remember that when staring into the soulless eyes of the Bogeyman.

He was only yards away, around the darkened corner. The scratchy sound of his breathing seemed to tap on her chest, threatening to end her at any second.

*He can't hurt me,* she told herself, but it did little to calm her. The fear of the monster that had scared children for eons was as real to Liv as the hairs standing up on the back of her neck.

However, the lore that surrounded the beast was murky

at best. There was no documentation of anyone ever being hurt by the Bogeyman, and yet there were numerous unsolved cases involving missing people that were loosely correlated to the monster.

This creature was a myth to some, a figure made up to scare children into staying in bed. Liv knew now that was absolutely false. He was real. She'd stared at the shadow-like black figure with her own eyes. If that was false, then what else was? Could he actually hurt her? Take her soul? Steal her away?

Plato had told her the trick for taking the Bogeyman down, but doing it was so much harder in reality. How could something so easy be so incredibly hard?

The scraping on the carpet at Liv's back grew closer. The Bogeyman was only feet away.

All Liv had to do was say five words. That was all. She didn't have to slay the beast using Bellator or have an exhausting and lethal battle with him. Just say five words. But she had to mean them. And right then, she knew that was impossible. The fear was too real.

Her heart thumped so loudly in her chest that it hurt. She wasn't even looking at the Bogeyman yet. When she had before, she'd nearly crumpled to her knees from the fear.

Unable to face him, she sprinted, feeling something claw at her heels as she took off. Liv didn't look back. Instead, she ran as if her life depended on it, not stopping until she rounded the corner in the dark building.

The fifty-story skyscraper was in New York City. It had no rooms, only hallways that traced around the building, going up and up and leading nowhere. It was the Bogey-man's home, a place few knew about besides Plato.

Most wouldn't willingly walk into the Bogeyman's lair since it would be like signing themselves up for an adrenaline rush that had killed many. Liv was reminded of that as she threw her back against the wall to the next bend and stared at a corpse that was more bones than rotting flesh.

She covered her nose and mouth against the horrid smell, but it was the expression of panic on the dead man's face that nearly made her vomit. Fear brought out the worst in people. It did horrible things to them, and the expectation of what was to come was worse than the actual experience.

Franklin Delano Roosevelt had once said, "The only thing we have to fear is fear itself."

Liv wondered if he had ever stood mere feet from the Bogeyman and listened to his rattling breath, which seemed to promise the cruelest of endings? Maybe if he had, he would have said, "The only thing we have to fear is fear itself…oh, and the Bogeyman. Run from that monster before it gets you."

Even her usual attempts at internal banter didn't help. She lifted her hand and found that she was violently vibrating, as if the floor under her was quaking badly. Liv glanced down. The floor was still. It was she who was trembling, and with each passing moment, it was getting worse.

She had to get control of herself. But first, she had to run.

Liv sprinted for the next bend, hopefully putting

enough space between her and the Bogeyman to buy her the time she needed to survive.

With her back pressed against the next wall, Liv took measured breaths. She'd learned from Akio, her combat instructor, that a one-to-two ratio activated the rest-and-restore sequence in the body. That was what she needed right then—a restoration of her mind, her emotions, and more importantly, her body. That was what the Bogeyman would measure when she said those five simple, magical words. He apparently could assess someone's physiology, like a monstrous lie detector. If she didn't mean those five words, he would know, and then it would be too late for a plan B.

Blowing out a breath, Liv closed her eyes and pictured herself in bed as a young child. She remembered experiencing the fear she was feeling now. She remembered feeling it when her bladder was full and the bathroom was a long fifteen feet away. Too many times, she'd thought she'd pee in the bed rather than simply make the walk across the darkened space. She forced herself to relive that memory now, speaking to her younger self.

*He doesn't own you,* she stated in her mind.

*He might be real, but the fear comes from your own imagination,* Liv stated definitively in her mind.

*The Bogeyman can't hurt you.*

She watched in her mind's eye as her younger self pushed her covers aside, swinging her feet over the bed. Little Liv nearly hiccupped on her breath as the soles of her feet touched the floor, like she expected something to grab her from under her bed.

*Don't fear him,* Adult Liv said loudly in her mind,

speaking over the scuttling sound of the Bogeyman drawing closer. She tried to stay focused.

Little Liv took a step forward, gauging the shadows all around her in the darkened room.

"There's nothing there," Liv said out loud for the dark building and the Bogeyman to hear.

In her mind, Little Liv continued toward the bathroom, not exhaling until she made it there unharmed.

Liv's eyes sprang open in the darkened corridor. To her surprise, her pulse was steady. Her breath, too. Her mind was clear of the exhausting fear that had been controlling her.

She nodded to the darkness like she'd made an agreement with it.

Then, without giving herself a moment to hesitate, she stepped around the corner and faced the long corridor she'd come down.

In the center, crawling along the tattered carpet, was the worst beast she'd ever seen. He was black and moved like a serpent along the floor, his yellow eyes wide and his mouthful of sharp, jagged teeth bared.

Liv lifted her chin and her hand at the same time, glaring straight into the soulless monster's eyes.

"I'm not scared of you!" she exclaimed, holding her hand up, her fingers spread wide.

Nothing happened for a long few seconds, and then the Bogeyman spiraled into blackness, a screech spilling from him that made her teeth hurt. He flew toward her hand, crumpling into her palm like a cobweb she'd swatted from a corner. When he was little more than wadded-up darkness in her hand, Liv pulled a bottle from her cape and slapped her palm on the top of it.

The clear bottle filled with blackness. Before the Bogeyman could escape, Liv stuck a cork in it, trapping the monster. He would be secure there until she'd put him in his new place for what would hopefully be the rest of time.

## CHAPTER TWO

Repairing the stairs that led to the gates to the underworld had taken both Liv's and Clark's efforts. That was because the magic under the craft mall in Canada was strong, meant to protect the entrance to such a powerful and strange place. However, Liv was going to need a way to get down there so that she could put the new guard in place. That was why they had to ensure the stairs were rebuilt, hopefully well enough to last this time.

The owner of the craft mall, Amity Buckwell, hadn't been upset when Liv had told her that major renovations needed to be done to the basement under her shop. She'd simply nodded and held up her hands. "Whatever you need to do to keep the ghosts locked away, simply do it."

Liv nodded, thinking it was better not to tell her that there weren't any ghosts under her shop, but rather a ton of lost souls who would love more than anything to escape the underworld. Mortals had come a long way in their understanding of magic, but there were still some things they didn't need to know about.

For instance, there was little reason to tell the good-natured Amity that a three-headed dog used to live under the craft mall. Further, there was absolutely *no* reason to tell her that it would be the new home of the Bogeyman.

"I had a dream last night that I went shopping at Target with Jack Nicholson," Liv told Plato as they descended the stairs. There was a nervous hum in her chest that she couldn't shake, maybe because they were nearing the underworld, which was currently unguarded, or maybe because she was holding the Bogeyman inside a glass bottle in her hands.

"What did you buy?" Plato asked casually, appearing as unnerved as she was. He had almost gotten sucked into this place due to his many attempts at avoiding death, and the potential of it happening again was strong. He looked worried.

"Really?" Liv questioned. "That's your follow up question? Not, why Jack Nicholson, or was he cool, or why did you go to Target, of all places?"

"I know all about Jack," Plato said smugly. "We've met… a few times."

"Of course you have." She rolled her eyes. "Are you bridge partners or something?"

"Maybe," he answered coyly. "And we're almost out of bubble bath."

Liv halted, blinking at the lynx. "Why are you telling me that right now?"

He shook his head at her. "Because you were just at Target. You could have picked up some."

Liv opened her mouth to reply but realized that it would be useless. She continued down the stairs to the cavernous cellar under the craft mall. "We wouldn't be out of bubble bath if *someone* didn't go through it so fast."

"I realize that you're insinuating it was me, but you're wrong," Plato stated. "Clark keeps blaming it on Sophia, but he's the one who takes two-hour-long baths with candles while eating decadent chocolates."

Liv grimaced. "Gross."

"I know, soapy hands don't mix well with eating chocolate."

"No," Liv argued. "I was commenting on the fact that you're spying on Clark in the bathtub."

"Oh, well, that was purely an accident, but when you've lived as long as me, you don't see things the same way as you young'uns. It's not spying, just entertainment."

"Don't watch me bathe, Plato," she warned.

"Thing is, you'd have to actually bathe for me to be able to do that," he countered.

"Oh, shush it. I bathe."

"*But* you don't wash behind your ears, and you think the water running down the drain is actually cleaning your feet."

Liv shook her head. "Somehow I'm putting an anti-lynx security system in the bathroom."

He shrugged. "You can try, but it doesn't work for most, I've found."

"You're very strange."

When they'd gotten to the bottom of the stairs, Liv stopped, staring at the gate Russ had knocked down. It was now securely in place again, although open. She and Clark had also placed charms on all the gates, reinforcing them for when the time came to lock it again.

"Are you sure the Bogeyman is the right guardian for the underworld?" Liv asked for like the millionth time.

"Of all our options, yes," Plato answered.

"What does that mean?" Liv questioned.

"Well, we could pick a unicorn or Pegasus or something like that, but the world would miss having those creatures in the mix," he explained. "The key is to pick something the world doesn't need roaming around and creating havoc. Here, the Bogeyman is actually doing a service, and as a bonus, he's not harassing young children or those like you who come to prey on him."

Liv nodded, remembering the reasoning now. "Okay, right. I'm doing a service. The Bogeyman will take Russ's place guarding the underworld and leave the innocent alone."

"Now, remember what you've got to do after you've placed him behind the fifth gate?" Plato quizzed.

"I believe you said, 'run like hell.'"

The lynx nodded. "Yes. I'll take care of the spell that assigns him as the guardian of the underworld."

"Since it should actually be you since you're the one who killed Russ, I'm passing the job on to you," Liv stated.

Plato lowered his head like someone could be listening. "It's not necessary to keep reminding those who could be listening of that, or that I'm not dead anymore."

Liv lowered her head too. "Who is listening?"

Plato drew in closer, his face near to hers. "You don't want to know."

Liv stood up, facing the open gate. "Fine, keep your secrets. I'm certain you're right."

"Are you ready?" Plato asked, sitting down.

"Aren't you coming?" Liv asked, over her shoulder.

He gave her a look, and she knew at once. Plato had magic to do, and it was better if she wasn't present for it. Her job was to deposit the Bogeyman and run. His job was to assign him and lock the gates behind her, not seeing Plato while he did it.

She nodded as she trekked farther into the darkness. "I'll holler when I'm ready."

"No need," Plato called. "I always know where you are and what you're doing even when I'm not watching."

"I won't remind you how creepy that is."

He chuckled. "I believe you just did."

When Liv reached the fifth gate, she let out a long breath, preparing herself for the next phase of the plan. It was easy. Uncork the bottle full of a being who was seemingly liquid ink at the moment. Spill him onto the dirt that was only yards away from the entrance to the underworld, where the worst and most horrible souls resided. Then run like her life depended on it...because it most assuredly did.

Liv tensed before pulling the cork from the bottle, a strange, guttural sound echoing up from the pits of hell below. She was able to finally pull her eyes away from the darkness below.

"Okay, here I go," she whispered to herself.

Plato's voice echoed from the entrance. "You got this."

Liv was grateful for the chuckle that escaped her mouth. It made the next part easier. She pulled the cork and threw the bottle straight into the seemingly endless blackness. Not far, but enough that it gave her some lead time. Then she took off running.

It wasn't five seconds later that she felt the tug on her

heels again, and the swooshing in her ears. The pull at her core. But as Plato had advised her, she didn't look back. Instead, she sprinted, throwing the first gate back and listening intently for the locking sound.

When it clicked, Liv's heart finally relaxed in her chest. She didn't slow, though. She continued running through the tunnel, shutting the other gates behind her. Each click gave her extra relief. She didn't stop until she'd thrown herself through the last gate and tumbled to the floor, covering her face from Plato, who she knew she couldn't look at right then, lest he lose a life.

When he did magic, he transformed, and simply seeing him would take a life from the lynx. He only had a hundred, and she wanted him to keep all of them for as long as possible, if not forever.

When the final gate was locked and the swirling in Liv's ears had dissipated, she dared to look up.

Plato was casually licking his paw in cat form and regarding her with a relaxed expression.

"Is everything okay?" she asked, looking around.

Plato lowered his paw and smiled. "I'm starving, and I suspect you are too, but yes. The underworld has a new guardian, whom I think will stay in place for a long time."

Liv smiled with relief, standing tall. "Well, that was easy."

Plato huffed. "And you had to say that, didn't you?"

"Oh, will you stop being so superstitious?" Liv asked.

He shook his head. "No, because you've totally jinxed us, and I wanted to stop off at that one place that has the spicy bean dip."

"And we will if you'll stop being so fussy. Everything is fine." Then she patted her sides. "Oh, wait…"

"What?" Plato asked, tension in his voice.

"Bellator. I must have dropped it…"

Plato's eyes widened. "I told you not to jinx us. Now we have to open the gates and do it all over, and the Bogeyman will get loose, and we'll have to risk—"

"Oh, you're so easy," Liv said with a laugh, striding up the new staircase, her head held high. "I didn't bring Bellator with me."

Plato didn't appear amused. "Just so you know, I'm telling Jack that you're a lousy shopping partner and a horrible conversationalist."

# CHAPTER THREE

Ever since trapping the Bogeyman, Liv couldn't shake the fear his presence had stirred. Yes, she'd overcome it to conquer him, but fear wasn't something one simply mastered forever. It was a back-and-forth race where sometimes she felt ahead of it, and at other times it overwhelmed her. For her, sometimes fear meant forgetting everything and running, and at other times, it stood for "face everything and rise."

Being a Warrior for the House of Fourteen had challenged Liv in ways she hadn't dreamt possible. She'd faced things that were beyond nightmares. She'd done things she used to hear her mother speak about, like facing down an army of madmen singlehandedly, and she was alive to tell the tale. She hoped that wherever Guinevere Beaufont was, she was proud of her.

Right then, Liv didn't know how to feel about her present life. Something was shifting inside her, and it strangely felt like an evolution. That meant change, and change was…hard.

But deep down, she knew that no matter what happened... Liv stopped in the middle of the sidewalk, making some hipsters with too much facial hair and bad reaction time run into her.

"Hey, Munchkin, watch it," one of the tall guys said, peeling around Liv like she was a linebacker who had nearly taken him out.

Liv glared at the jerks with their rolled-up jeans and brand new t-shirts that they'd bought with holes. "Why don't you watch where you're going, or I'll toss you across the yellow brick road."

The guy shook his head and exchanged irritated expressions with his friend. "She's the one who works at that electronics repair shop down the block."

His buddy slapped his arm. "Apparently, the electronics aren't the only things with a screw loose."

Liv knew better than to mess with mortals. However, she had no problem punishing assholes. Discreetly pointing her finger at the two guys, she muttered a single word. Both of their beards disappeared, and their clothes were replaced by starched khakis and pressed Polo shirts.

"What the hell?" the first guy yelled, running his hands over his chin. "It took me a year to grow that beard. What the hell happened to it?"

The other guy gawked at his friend's appearance before looking down at his own. "Seriously, where are our clothes? We look like...our parents."

"Now go get real jobs, boys," Liv called, jaywalking across the street. "Because podcasting and posting pictures of your food on Instagram aren't professions."

The guys strode off, looking dazed as they glanced

down at their outfits. This left her wondering about the thought that had made her pause in the first place.

*Deep down...*

Lately, that phrase kept surfacing, and it was always followed by the idea that things were going to be okay. On the surface, there was all this fear about the future, the people she loved, and her ever-changing role as a Warrior for the House. However, after dwelling on these worries, Liv always found herself shrugging and thinking, "Deep down, I know everything will be okay."

*Why?* she found herself thinking as she walked on. What was in this deep down place in her that had so much confidence? And how could she spend more of her time there instead of wrestling with fears and worries? Liv didn't know, but she hoped to find out.

What she needed right then was to throw herself into some repair project at the shop. Only when she was fixing things did her immediate concerns not overwhelm her. She didn't ponder Sophia's future or wonder if she and Stefan would ever be together or worry that Rory was never going to find happiness or that Rudolf was probably putting his finger in an electrical socket.

Taking a deep breath, Liv threw open the shop door, expecting that familiar smell of metal and rust that always filled John's shop.

But it was gone.

Liv halted, looking around at the repair shop, which was cleaner than she'd ever seen it. Strangely, she could have sworn a few sparkles radiated off the shelves as she looked around.

For a full minute, Liv stood completely still, wondering

if she'd walked into the electronics repair shop in the wrong dimension. That had always been a warped concern of hers, although she was pretty sure it was impossible…probably.

John's laughter broke her daze as he strode through the door to the back carrying a record player some hipster had dropped off for repair. They loved their vinyl these days. She could make a killing repairing typewriters and selling them to the West Hollywood crowd, who liked vintage things over practical ones.

"You tell me what your favorite Beatles' song is first," he said over his shoulder.

Alicia strode in behind him, carrying a turntable. "How about I play it for you," she stated, and on the old jukebox Liv had gotten for John, the song, *I Want to Hold Your Hand* began playing.

John smiled broadly, his attention on the scientist beside him. "I like it. One of my favorites, too."

"But not your ultimate favorite?" Alicia questioned. Neither her nor John noticed that Liv was standing just inside the shop.

Flicking her finger at the jukebox, Liv switched the song to *Hey Jude*.

John and Alicia exchanged curious expressions, still not noticing Liv. They didn't seem to see anything but each other.

"That's John's favorite Beatles' song," Liv said, strangely finding her voice grumpy.

The two swung around. Alicia yelped, put down the turntable, and ran over to hug her.

John simply beamed. "She's absolutely right. Liv knows

me best. That's my favorite song."

Liv released Alicia, feeling unlike her usual self. "Why is the shop so clean?"

Alicia looked her over. "I heard about all your recent adventures from John. He was so proud of you. I am too, and I'm glad you're looking well."

Liv forced a smile, running her eyes over the pristine shelves. "Thanks. Are the brownies working overtime?"

Alicia followed her gaze. "Oh, no. I just decided to tidy up since I had some spare time."

"Looks nice, doesn't it?" John asked, proudly glancing around the shop.

"Looks sterile," Liv snapped bitterly. She wasn't sure of the reason for her sudden sour mood. Something was going on inside her that she wasn't completely aware of, and she didn't like that at all. Maybe she needed to walk back and forth through the Door of Reflection a few times until she'd emptied herself of all her buried demons.

John chuckled. "That was my reaction at first. I'm used to a few dust bunnies here and there, but I could get used to the clean smell. It sure keeps my allergies at bay."

Liv sighed as Plato entered through the still-open door at the back and strode over to her. He rubbed against her leg, looking spritely and young, which was still taking some getting used to every time she looked at him. "Yeah, I guess you have a point. Good job, Alicia. It's just different than I'm used to, and I was hoping for a bit of nostalgia after my last mission."

Alicia and John exchanged looks of concern.

Liv waved them off before they could offer her their

sympathy. "I'm fine. Just had to battle the Bogeyman and stick him at the entrance to hell."

John winked at Alicia. "When she used to say things like that, I thought she was kidding or exaggerating, but after being on the council, I realize she's probably downplaying everything." He pointed to Plato. "Unlike with the cat she keeps trying to convince me talks."

"He does," Liv said dryly.

John laughed like this was at all a joke.

"Doesn't he look a bit younger than before?" Liv argued.

"Well, yeah," John stated, slapping his knee. Pickles immediately bounded out of the back, yapping and excited, in terrier form. "But that's not very impressive. Magical creatures can change. Just look at Pickles."

On cue, the dog switched to chimera form, his small head transformed into that of a lion and the rest of him changing as well.

"But you don't think that Plato can talk?" Liv asked, lowering her chin.

John patted Pickles on the head. "Some things are just too hard to believe. I guess I'd have to see it."

Liv snapped at the lynx. "Speak, boy."

Plato yawned, settling down on his paws and laying his head down. He appeared to be about to take an impromptu nap.

Both John and Alicia laughed like this was all a part of a well-rehearsed skit.

"Fine," Liv declared. "The cat can't talk. I'm ready to work. What projects have we had come in today?"

"They are all done," John stated proudly.

"Oh, really?" Liv asked in disbelief. "So not much, then?"

"Oh, tons," he answered. "Business is booming. But Alicia took care of them already."

"Well, any bigger things I can work on? Like a washing machine or something?"

John thought for a moment and then shook his head. "No, we are all caught up."

Liv drooped slightly with disappointment. Everything was changing, and she should be happy. The electronics repair shop was clean, successful, and the work done. However, it left her feeling unneeded and helpless. If she wasn't repairing stuff in her spare time, what would she do?

The thought was so strange and arresting that she felt herself sway. If John didn't need her, she'd have to be a full-time Warrior. That job demanded more than enough time from her, but she had never expected to do it solely. For some reason, holding onto her old life while she pretended to be a mortal had always grounded her. Upon entering the shop a few minutes prior, she'd looked forward to the distractions that repairing electronics gave her. The peace. But if she didn't have it there anymore...then she'd have to find it somewhere else. Maybe inside her. That was a weird thought.

Liv turned suddenly, looking out at the street, unsure of why it had attracted her attention. She wasn't really studying the street and passing cars, but rather the idea of "out there." Somewhere out there was a world she thought needed her more than the repair shop. That wasn't a comforting thought. It brought more fears.

And with that thought came another one. *Somewhere out*

*there was something besides the repair shop that could bring her peace.*

But Liv had no idea what that might be.

However, things were plain enough for her to see inside the walls of her old sanctuary as the Beatles' music played from the jukebox and John and Alicia giggled together, obviously forgetting she was still there.

She wasn't needed there anymore. That should be a good thing.

John was happy, and she loved him like a father.

Alicia was happy, and Liv loved her like an old friend.

The shop was prospering, and she loved this place like…well, it *was* her home.

However, neither John nor Alicia nor the shop needed her right then, and that was a good thing, she told herself.

Wasn't life about giving the ones you loved enough space that they could be happy on their own? Helping others find their way? That was what her job as a Warrior was, essentially. When she'd completed each successful mission, she'd never been sad for the happy ending.

When Liv had helped Renswick Shoshawnawalla overcome the demons who had taken his wife, she didn't mourn. When she'd helped Rooster, the musician, repair his fractured heart, she hadn't been sad. When she'd helped Fane, the new alpha of the original werewolf pack, protect his own, Liv hadn't been remorseful. And yet, it was hard for her to suddenly realize that the repair shop would be fine without her. John didn't need her, and she needed to move on.

Deep down, she knew this was a good thing, but she wanted to curse this place inside her that seemed to know things Because right then, Liv wanted her old life back. She wanted things to be like they always had.

John's sincere laughter brought her back to reality. He leaned down and was about to kiss Alicia on the cheek, but his eyes suddenly whipped up to find Liv watching them.

She bowed her head and turned for the door. "I've got to go check on Sophia. I'll see you at the House later, John."

Liv didn't wait for his reply before bolting out the front door, feeling heavy and yet strangely happy. She was confounded by her new emotional state. How could she be happy for the ones she loved, and also remorseful for herself at the same time?

All she knew for sure was that her life was changing. Everything was evolving.

And if she could live in the deep-down place, the fear of the what-ifs and the future wouldn't constantly try to monopolize her attention.

CHAPTER FOUR

L*iv was going to be mad,* Sophia Beaufont thought as she glanced at her image in the pond beside her dragon's egg.

*No, she's going to be sad,* the dragon she hadn't named yet replied in her head.

*She's going to be devasted,* Sophia amended.

*She'll get over it,* the dragon stated matter-of-factly, no sympathy in his voice.

You're *going to get over it,* Sophia spat, realizing she was being immature, which was ironic since she'd aged roughly five years in the last hour. It hadn't been like the other times, where she simply woke up and was taller. It was excruciatingly painful feeling her bones grow rapidly and her skin stretch to cover them.

She panted now from the exhaustion of rapidly growing, waiting for her magical reserves to return after the ordeal so she could fix her outfit. Her dress was now several inches too short and pinching her waistline miserably.

Her dragon, once again, hadn't been very sympathetic, simply stating, *Join the club.* Apparently, that was how growing had been for him most of the time, except he had to sprout horns and sharp claws, which was supposedly really exhausting and painful.

*That was your comeback?* the dragon asked. *You just simply fired back at me that I'll get over it? I have nothing to get over. I'm the one who pushed for the rapid growth. That joke didn't make any sense.*

*It was the first thing I could think of,* Sophia stated, crossing her arms over her chest and finding the experience much different than before. She had boobs! She'd matured a lot.

*Growing those still wasn't more painful than growing horns,* dragon shot back, having read her thoughts of disbelief. There was no privacy from him, and he had said that was for the best. Between dragon and rider, there were never any secrets.

Sophia turned to face the shimmering blue egg, which was much larger now too. "What do you mean, you pushed for the rapid growth?" she asked aloud.

*The time was right since we're together, and we don't have many opportunities anymore because you only visit every other day,* he explained.

Sophia sighed, realizing he was right. She'd had to stay away from her dragon's egg for days at a time in order to hide his presence from the Elite. When Sophia and her dragon were together, their magic pulsed on the Elite's radar like a nuclear blast. Having him at Rory's, where he was content, helped a little. The real trick to hiding them was having the giants around—Rory, Maddie, and

Bermuda. Their magic was able to skew the normal signals a dragon and rider broadcast for the Elite to pick up.

Sophia'd had mixed feelings when Liv had told her she wanted to hide them from the Elite for a little while. The future dragon rider had thought it might be time that she joined her own and brought her dragon into the presence of his elders. Currently, he had no influences who were dragons. She wasn't sure that was a good thing, but he'd said he didn't mind.

It had actually been the dragon who had said that Liv was right. Once he hatched, there would be no hiding them, he'd told Sophia. The Elite would show up and take them away. They'd be stunned since a new dragon hadn't hatched in over a hundred years, and there would be other things that shocked them, like Sophia being a girl and so young.

Riders had always been male up until this point. Since her dragon was born with a genetic memory of the dragons' history, he had known this before Rory had told them.

Further, most eggs didn't magnetize to a rider until they were much, much older, like by a half a century or more. That was because dragons wanted their riders to be mature, having had life experiences to complement the dragon's immediate maturity once hatched.

But the dragon had said Sophia was different. Not an old soul, per se, but apparently she had a grasp on magic that far exceeded the expectations for someone her age. She'd known that for a while, having had to hide her magic from the House of Fourteen to avoid registering it and starting lessons.

Her education had taken on a more organic form,

SARAH NOFFKE & MICHAEL ANDERLE

allowing her to go at her own pace. She hadn't wanted that to stop, but as soon as someone on the council found out she had magic, there would be controls and boundaries. Sophia was different from her brother Clark in that she didn't like rules. They always made her feel congested, and she awkwardly resisted them.

Because she'd magnetized to the egg at such a young age, she'd had to go through rapid aging. Otherwise, the egg would have to wait to hatch until she caught up with him. Sophia had told the dragon that she didn't want to wait seven or eight years. She reminded herself as they stood in the dragon's oasis in Rory's backyard that she'd asked for this. She'd willingly given up a chunk of her childhood to have her dragon early. Later there might be some regrets around this, she suspected, but for now, she was excited that soon she'd be able to meet her dragon face to face. She couldn't imagine having to wait close to a decade for that experience.

*You are full-grown now,* dragon explained to her.

Sophia glanced down and magicked a new outfit that fit much better than the dress. For some reason, she didn't feel like wearing one of her usual frilly garments. Instead, she opted for a pair of tight-fitting pants like Liv always wore and an armored top that was light and flexible. Maybe she'd picked this outfit because there was something pulsing in her chest, making her feel like running, jumping, fighting.

*The chi of the dragon has awoken inside you,* the dragon stated.

"The what?" she asked.

*It is the spirit that bonds us as dragon and rider,* he

explained. *It makes you stronger, faster, and all-around better than any normal magician. It increases your life expectancy tenfold. And it ensures that no matter where you go, I can always find you.*

"Since I'm full-grown now, does that mean you're going to hatch soon?" Sophia asked the egg.

She pictured his shrug in her mind's eye. *Maybe*, he replied. *Within the year.*

Sophia sighed. "Can't you speed it up a bit?"

Although Sophia wasn't looking forward to leaving her friends and family, a part of her didn't feel complete as long as her dragon was still in his shell. She realized that even though her body had matured, she still had the mind of a nine-year-old. Usually, a girl her age would want to stay as close to their family as possible, but Sophia was a very different child. She had been selected for something unique, and she wasn't afraid of where it was going to take her, although something told her she should be.

*Speed is good in battle, but it shouldn't be employed in development,* the dragon told her. *I'll hatch when I'm ready, and when I sense that you are.*

"I have hips," Sophia argued. "I think I'm ready!"

She sensed the dragon shake his head. That was how it worked with them. She could feel him when he wasn't around. Knew his reactions without seeing him. And felt his mood, which usually made knowing her own confusing if they were on opposite sides of the spectrum.

*You aren't ready*, dragon replied. *And more importantly, neither are the ones who love you most.*

Sophia huffed. "My childhood ended an hour ago. I think the ones who love me are going to get ready pretty fast. I skipped the 'tween years and was launched straight into being a teenager in minutes."

*Is that why you're being so unruly?* her dragon asked.

Sophia rolled her eyes.

*I saw that,* dragon stated at once.

"I'm going through a lot all of a sudden. That's why I'm being this way," she explained.

*Horns,* he barked in her head. *Once again,* you *didn't have to grow horns.*

"And you didn't just bypass puberty and land smack-dab in the center of womanhood!"

*I'll remind you that what you experience, I do too, so I know a little bit about what you're going through,* the dragon informed her evenly.

"Oh, good," Sophia joked. "The boy dragon is going to relate to how it feels to be a woman. This should be interesting."

*Tonight is the full moon,* he said casually, as if mentioning this at all related to what they were talking about.

"Thanks, I'll let my werewolf friends know."

*You don't know any werewolves,* he replied. *And I'm telling you that because you'll be impacted more by the full moon. It was why I chose today to rapidly age you, but it will heighten your emotions.*

"So don't go outside?" Sophia asked.

*And stay away from people as much as a possible,* he advised. *Otherwise, you might regret the things you say to them.*

Sophia nodded, feeling irrational emotions build inside her. "Why did you pick the full moon for this?"

*Each dragon has a special connection to Earth,* her dragon offered. *Some are influenced by seasons, others by the tides, and there are a thousand other ways. My power is tied to the moon. It can make both of us stronger or weaker, depending on its state.*

Sophia nodded, realizing this was incredibly important. She wasn't sure exactly how yet, but something told her that one day, the dragon's connection to the moon would either save them or put them in mortal danger...or both.

# CHAPTER FIVE

"You're feeling sorry for yourself," Plato observed as they neared Rory's house.

"I am not," Liv argued, wishing her voice didn't sound so dejected.

"Well, I guess I would feel similarly in your situation," Plato stated matter-of-factly.

"My situation?" Liv argued. "I don't have a situation. I'm just a girl with a sword and a job to do. There is no situation."

"Right, and John not needing your help at the electronics shop doesn't bother you at all," Plato countered.

"I mean, it's different, but I'm happy for him. And for Alicia. They seem joyful, like they are in the honeymoon phase without having gotten married."

"Sure," Plato offered. "But that doesn't mean you don't feel left out. I know how much repairing stuff relaxes you."

"It's fine. It gives me more time to work on my tan and brush up on my French," Liv stated.

"*Comment se fait-il que ton cul pâle ne connaisse pas le sort de l'apprentissage des langues étrangères ?*" Plato asked.

"I sense you've just said something about my paleness," Liv said, looking down at the lynx.

He shrugged. "*Peut-être.*"

"Well, the next time we're at that French market on Sunset Boulevard, why don't you try ordering for me?" Liv suggested.

"I would, but they'd still mix up your order since a talking cat usually unnerves people, even those who are used to the magical world."

Liv rolled her eyes. "And *that's* why you won't talk in front of John?"

He snickered. "Oh, no. That's purely because I like torturing you."

"You're such a kind and gentle soul."

Plato nodded. "And then there's the whole Sophia situation."

Liv huffed. "That's not bothering me. So what if my baby sister has a dragon egg that's about to hatch and she will be whisked away to a secret society and I'll never see her again? I'm totally fine with that. Do you want sushi for dinner?"

Plato shot her a sly expression. "Since when have you started eating sushi?"

"Since I quit caring what I put in my mouth," she said, her defeat rising to the surface.

"And that's because you're upset about the shop and Sophia, and then there's the whole Stefan thing," Plato observed.

Liv halted. "There is nothing with Stefan. We're better than ever."

"Even though you can't be together?" Plato questioned.

"Yes," she argued, continuing the trek to Rory's house. "Because then he'd come around all the time and make me laugh, and we'd probably get fat together since that's what couples do when they are in love. And my job would suffer, which means the whole world would quickly go to hell. So yes, us not being together is for the best."

"I believe you said the L-word," Plato casually observed.

"Well, he does make me laugh. More than most people, anyway. And usually I'm laughing with him, not at him, which is also rare."

"Yes, 'laugh.'" Plato nodded. "That's the L word I was referring to."

"Anyway, so what if there are a lot of changes going on in my life?" Liv said. "And maybe I'm feeling a little bit down about it all."

"You know, you can laugh in the rain, or you can cry, but you're going to get wet regardless."

Liv looked at the clear blue sky. "I don't know what you're talking about. It's not going to rain."

Plato shook his head. "It's raining on you right now."

Liv continued to gaze at the cloudless sky, trying to hide the emotions prickling to the surface. When she finally felt steady enough to reply, she said, "Well, I hope it stops raining soon, but I'll try to laugh about it until it does."

"Cutting back on the hallucinogens might also help," Bermuda said from the front porch.

Liv brought her chin down to find the giantess holding

a broom in one hand and the other on her hip. Plato had unsurprisingly disappeared, making her look like she was talking to herself. "Oh, I realize that it's not raining. I was having a metaphorical conversation."

Bermuda looked around blankly. "With whom?"

"Hallucinogens," Liv agreed with a sigh. "I'll cut back on them."

Bermuda nodded as she began sweeping the front porch, although it appeared perfectly clean.

"Is Rory here?" Liv asked, sensing a new tension in the giantess. She needed to cross the porch to the front door but thought Bermuda might try to sweep her feet out from under her.

"He is," she stated flatly.

"Oh, great. Is he busy?"

"Apparently," Bermuda replied at once, her eyes on her work.

"Well, Sophia mentioned that she'd be stopping by later. I was hoping to catch her. Do you know if she's here?" Liv asked.

"I don't think so," Bermuda answered.

"Maybe I'll just wait in the front yard until she gets here."

The giantess stopped sweeping and glared at Liv, a long, hard look that seemed to try to cut her from the inside out. "You meddled."

Liv opened her mouth, ready to defend herself. To tell Bermuda that Rory shouldn't be belittled for his choices. And that Maddie was a nice person. And that she was tired of being bullied by the giantess. But she suddenly found herself unable to speak. Her lips moved, but no noise came out. Liv grabbed her throat, wondering what was wrong with her.

Bermuda actually smiled, but only a little. "I know how you like to talk, and that will make what I've got to say a lot harder. Forgive me for putting a silencing spell on you. It's nothing I like doing to others, but for you, it's sort of an improvement, if I do say so myself."

Liv dropped her hands from her throat and tilted her head to the side, shooting the giantess an annoyed expression.

"Now," Bermuda began, taking a step forward, the broom in tow, "it has come as quite a shock to me to find that my Rory didn't like running the family accounting business."

*Oh, the jokes Liv would tell if only she could speak...*

"And, then there was the matter of this girl you dragged into our home under the ruse that she'd help with the dragon's egg," Bermuda continued.

The giantess was right. It was better that Liv couldn't talk. Otherwise, she would have interrupted her several times already and probably wound up with a black eye or something.

"Since I met you, Liv Beaufont, you've been..." Bermuda stopped, chewing on her lip as if wrestling internally to identify the right word.

Liv could have helped supply some options if she could speak.

"You've been a complete and utter pain in the rear end," Bermuda stated, her fingers turning white around the broom handle.

Liv nodded. *Yes, this conversation was going exactly as expected.*

"You've brought that lynx around here, who is entirely sneaky, in my opinion," Bermuda stated. "And you gave my Rory all these ideas that make him rebel against me. And then you brought other questionable people around, like Rudolf, who I never would have allowed to set foot on our property. And if that wasn't enough, now we have a dragon's egg in our backyard, which is a drain on our magic to keep hidden from the Elite. Oh, and this isn't even to mention all the danger you put us in when you sought to uncover the Mortal Seven and go up against Adler Sinclair."

Liv simply tilted her head back and forth and shrugged. What else was she going to do when she couldn't say anything?

"Do you know what our lives were like before you came along?" Bermuda asked, pausing long and hard as if Liv could answer.

*Smooth? Safe? Less annoying?* Liv wondered.

"Boring," Bermuda answered.

Liv leaned back, thinking she might fall over.

"I did my work and kept my head down and my mouth shut," Bermuda explained. "I knew about the Mortal Seven, but I was unwilling to investigate, afraid Adler would make good on his threats. I wrote my books and made Rory run the business, and we refused to talk to anyone outside our circle because that is how giants operate. I had convinced myself it was for the best. It kept us safe. I believed it kept us happy."

Liv squinted at the giantess, wondering if she should

run. She couldn't speak, but she still had the use of her legs. She knew for a fact that Bermuda preferred boring, and Liv had messed with that balance by "meddling." She eyed the broom in her hand, wondering if she might need to pull Bellator out to defend herself if she didn't run.

"And then you came along with your big mouth and ideas you planted in Rory's head and all your strange friends."

Liv's eyes slid around. Maybe if she ran, she could get far enough away to open a portal and escape before the giantess caught her.

Bermuda set the broom against the side of the house and took a step forward, the sun cascading down her face making her appear strangely ominous. "I understand you've helped the lynx gain another hundred lives."

Liv took a small step backward, hoping Bermuda wouldn't notice it.

"And before that, you helped Rudolf to defeat the queen of the fae, and now he's a king," Bermuda said, taking a step down the stairs of the porch, which made the wood groan under her.

Liv took another step back.

"And Rory has officially quit the family business," Bermuda stated, her voice rising in intensity. "He's turned it over to my sister's children."

*Okay, it was time to run,* Liv thought. However, she found that her feet didn't want to move. Instead, she stood tall, facing the giantess. Bermuda was right about everything. Liv *had* meddled. She'd put the Laurens family in danger. She'd dragged them into every one of her affairs. Whatever happened next, Liv deserved. She braced herself for whatever the giantess was about to do to her.

"Liv, if it wasn't for you..." Bermuda shook her head, her face showing the internal war being waged inside. "What I'm trying to tell you is that if it wasn't for you... well, our lives wouldn't be so rich and wonderful."

Liv was utterly speechless, both because she'd been spelled, and also because she had no clue how to respond to that statement.

"I know what you must be thinking right now," Bermuda said, lowering her chin and shaking her head.

*No, I don't think you do,* Liv thought.

"If it wasn't for you, I might not have seen a different side of Plato," the giantess began, her face softening. "Rory tells me he lost his last life saving you. That is not how the lynxes I've known behaved. And then there's Rudolf. To most, he appears to be a bumbling idiot, but you somehow helped bring out the hero in him. And although I know he has a long road ahead of him, I think he could be a great king to the fae one day. And while Maddie wasn't my first choice to help our family, well, she's open-minded and free-spirited, which aren't terms I've ever used to describe a fellow giant. And you know what?"

Liv opened her mouth to respond but quickly realized the spell hadn't been lifted, so she simply shrugged.

"She makes Rory smile more often than I've ever seen him do," Bermuda stated. "Very much like Maddie, Rory isn't like most giants either. Those two, well, they might be good for each other."

Liv wanted to jump for joy, but she made her face remain stony.

"And then there's the accounting business," Bermuda continued. "Well, I'm still trying to process that, and I'm not afraid to admit I'm madder than hell about the whole thing. Rory tells me you instigated it all, encouraging him to quit."

*Thanks, Rory,* Liv thought. *I'll haunt you after your mum kills me.*

"I'm so furious that…" Bermuda's face turned a deep shade of red. She stomped, making the ground under Liv's feet quake. "I mean, I hadn't seen any of this about my son. I've never been so mad at myself in all my life."

Of all the things Liv hadn't expected Bermuda to say, that was the biggest one. Her lips formed the word, "What?"

Bermuda nodded. "It's true, and hard for me to admit. I've been so busy telling my son how to live his life and disapproving of every one of his decisions that I didn't even see how miserable he was. But now that he's turned over the family business, well, he's happy. I see how different he is, and it's all because of you. If it wasn't for you Liv, the Mortal Seven wouldn't have been recovered, the House wouldn't have changed, and so much would be the way it has for centuries."

Liv wasn't sure if it was too early to open her arms to Bermuda, offering her a hug.

The giantess' face changed again to pure frustration. "I mean, you're still highly annoying with your constant sarcasm and total disregard for proper dress."

*Maybe it* was *too soon to hug,* Liv thought, taking another step back.

"But I realize those are small things, and although I

won't make any promises, I'll work on being more accepting of you in that regard," Bermuda stated, her mood calming once more. "What I'm trying to say is thank you."

Liv coughed suddenly, surprised by the sound that erupted from her mouth. Bermuda must have taken off the silencing spell. Not wanting to ruin the moment, Liv simply nodded. "Well, thank you. You didn't have to say all that."

"And if I hadn't silenced you, I daresay I wouldn't have been able to," Bermuda stated, her face serious, but a smile dancing in her eyes.

"Well, I hope to continue to bring good things to your and Rory's lives," Liv said. "He's my friend, and I only want you both to be happy."

The giantess looked at her meaningfully before lifting her chin to the sky. "Yes, I think I'd like the same for you. Hopefully, the rain will stop for you soon."

Liv realized that it was best to quit while she was ahead. "Yes, I hope so. Thank you, Mrs. Laurens." She stepped around her and headed for the front door.

"Bermuda," the giantess said from behind her.

Liv halted, turning around. "I'm sorry, what did you say?"

"Call me Bermuda," she explained. "I mean, I know you and Rory are friends, but maybe after everything, you can start to think of me as one too."

Liv smiled. "I'd like that. Thanks, Bermuda."

## CHAPTER SIX

The sound of humming greeted Liv's ears when she entered the Laurens' house. Maddie popped her head around the corner, smiling at her from the kitchen.

"Hi, there! How are you, Liv?"

"I'm great," she lied. "What smells so good?"

"Oh, it's my secret family recipe for cornbread," Maddie stated. "I thought I'd whip up a batch while Mrs. Laurens is cleaning and Rory is working. I can't have anyone learning the ingredients or Papa would be furious."

"Does that change if they become family?" Liv dared to ask.

The giantess blushed, making the freckles on her nose stand out. "Well, I guess it would. But it's not like...I mean, I hadn't really..."

Liv waved her off. "Sorry, I have this way of saying things that makes others uncomfortable. Just ask anyone. Anyway, forget I said anything."

"Are you looking for Rory?" Maddie asked.

"Is Sophia here?" Liv questioned.

"I don't think so," Maddie stated. "But Rory is in the back."

"Thanks," Liv said, striding toward the hallway. She had never been back to the bedroom area and realized there was a small office after poking her head into several different bedrooms.

Rory was hunched over an old desk, squinting at a computer. On the wall over the desk were several cork-boards with images clipped from magazines. Lying in the corner were calendars and other papers that looked to be related to taxes.

"So you told your mum I was behind this whole-giving-up-the-family-business thing," Liv said, crossing her arms over her chest and glaring at the giant.

He looked up suddenly as if she'd brought him out of deep thought. "What? Oh, that. Well, yeah."

Liv simply continued to stare at him, doing her best to look angry.

"Well, it was the truth," he argued, throwing up his hands. "And she's already mad at you for…existing, so I figured—"

"I'd be your scapegoat," Liv interrupted.

"No, it's not that," Rory stated. "But things are tense with her right now. I mean, Maddie being here sort of sets her off, and then there is all the pressure from the changes in the magical world. The elves don't want to conform to the House of Fourteen laws and have been pulling the giants into the negotiations since we've never followed their rule. It's making for a lot of tension."

Liv couldn't keep up the act any longer. She allowed the relieved laughter she'd been harboring since talking with

Bermuda to fall out of her mouth. "Rory, it's fine. Your mum and I had a nice conversation. Well, not much of a back and forth conversation as much as her talking and me being the best listener ever."

His head rocked back on his neck in disbelief. "I'd have to see that to believe it."

"I listen," Liv argued, pretending to be offended.

"Anyway, I'm sorry I placed the brunt of the blame on you," Rory said, not appearing as somber as usual. There was actually a new light in his eyes. "It's been hard for me to stand up to my mum in the past because, well…"

"She's intimidating as hell?" Liv supplied.

He nodded. "Yes, and I didn't want to disappoint her. But you do what you want, and it works for you. And I don't know…I guess you've sort of had an influence on me."

Liv didn't know what to do with all this praise from the giants. It made the constant rain showers over her feel more like a light mist. She indicated his laptop. "What are you working on?"

Rory immediately blushed. "It's nothing. Just something silly."

She leaned over his shoulder and read the first line of the document on his screen. "Wars are won by a wink, a gesture, or an event that transpired a millennium before the battle. Humanity has always been saved by small acts, the ones where someone gained a piece of their own puzzle, not the ones where a hero stood prodigious on a battlefield."

Rory had actually sat back in his chair and allowed Liv

to read, although his back was tensed the entire time and his face pinched with nervousness.

She pulled her eyes away from the screen and glanced at her friend. "Rory, that's good. Is this the book you're writing?"

He nodded. "Yeah."

"What's it about?" Liv asked.

He blushed again, closing the screen so she could no longer read. "It's nothing. Just about this young girl."

"Young girl?" Liv questioned.

"Well, young adult, I guess," he amended.

Liv encouraged him, nodding. "Go on."

"I haven't been working on the book that long," he stated, eyes cast down. "The main character has been thrown into this role she doesn't want in this society of uptight people. But over the course of the series, she finds a place to belong and enjoys the challenges, even though they are deadly."

Liv lowered her chin. "Sounds strangely familiar."

Rory pushed back, pretending to search the bookshelf next to his desk. "Does it? Oh, well, it all came to me in a dream."

"I guess I should have assumed you'd write young adult," Liv said, her tone more sensitive now, realizing how uncomfortable he was.

"You did? Why?" he questioned.

"I don't know," Liv answered, studying the boards above his desk that had pictures and quotes pinned to them. "You're sensitive and tuned in. It just makes sense."

He sighed loudly. "I don't know. Writing fiction doesn't

make any sense to me. All I've ever known was accounting."

"Really?" Liv argued. "You have more hobbies than anyone I know. I think you writing a book makes *more* sense than anyone else I know trying to do it."

Rory gazed at her hopefully. "Really?"

Liv nodded. "Yes, and I appreciate that you're being audit that you want to be."

He shook his head. "Oh, wow. I should have expected that joke."

"You really should have." Liv's eyes jerked to the window behind Rory's desk, noticing how the backyard had suddenly grown dark. She peered out, spying a large raincloud that strangely hovered overhead. "That's weird."

"What's weird?" he asked.

Liv was about to point to the ominous raincloud over the yard when something next to the pond caught her attention. Standing next to the large, blue dragon's egg was a…woman.

Liv snapped to attention, her heart racing. She and Rory looked at each other, fear in their eyes as they realized a stranger had snuck into his yard and was inches from Sophia's dragon's egg.

# CHAPTER SEVEN

Liv yanked Bellator from its sheath as she sprinted for the backyard. She nearly ran into Maddie as she bolted through the kitchen, but was able to avoid her as she ducked under the pan of cornbread the giantess was holding, taken straight from the hot oven.

Without a moment's hesitation, Liv busted through the back door and hopped the rail, headed straight for the poacher or whoever had managed to break into the Laurens' yard.

When the figure spun, Liv halted, feeling as though she'd been kicked in the stomach. For several seconds she couldn't breathe as she stared into the face of the person in front of her. Bellator clattered from her hands, and for the second time that day, she thought she'd fall over. That was why she was grateful when Rory, having rushed out behind her, clapped a firm hand on her shoulder, seemingly to hold her up.

"It's okay, Liv," he said from behind her.

Liv shook her head. "Did you know?"

"No," he answered, his voice shocked as they stared at the woman beside the dragon's egg.

"Liv, it's me," her sister's voice assured her from only a few yards away. It didn't sound like Sophia, though. Not the Sophia she'd said goodbye to that morning, not realizing that the next time she'd see her, she'd have aged rapidly.

"I know it's you," Liv said, realizing her voice was trembling. "But what... I mean, why? How" is the most appropriate question, actually."

Bermuda and Maddie rushed out behind them. Liv turned to see them both halt next to Rory, their eyes wide with shock at the sight before them.

"Well, I should have seen this coming," Bermuda said, taking several more steps until she was just in front of Liv.

"*This?*" Liv questioned. "Is *this* normal?"

Bermuda shook her head. "Nothing about Sophia Beaufont and her dragon's egg is normal. She's defying every odds at this turn."

"Then how should you have seen this coming?" Liv asked, realizing her voice was bordering on hostile. How could she not be? Her little sister had aged several years since she saw her earlier that day.

She suddenly felt like she'd been incarcerated and lost time with Sophia, but then she reminded herself that it wasn't that long ago that she'd left her sister and her other siblings, not feeling that she could confine herself to the magical world any longer after her parents' death.

But Liv *had* come back. She'd devoted herself to her family, and now she'd lost more time. It was too much, but maybe it was absolutely what she deserved, she told herself, feeling the coolness in the air as the raincloud overhead darkened.

Bermuda took a step backward, glancing at Liv. "Your sister has to evolve to keep up with her dragon. As he grows, so must she."

Liv swallowed, wanting to rush over to her sister while feeling like she wasn't actually her baby sister anymore. Maybe she didn't know the girl before her like she had this morning. That thought constricted the air in her throat.

Bermuda studied the uncertainty in Liv's eyes, and to her surprise, she laid her large giantess' hand on the Warrior's shoulder as she passed her.

Briefly, she leaned over and whispered in Liv's ear. "She's the same person. Nothing has changed about her except the way she looks."

"But how can that be?" Liv asked, staring at the giant.

Bermuda glanced at Sophia and then Liv, a soft smile on her face. "Because Sophia Beaufont was always ahead of her time. She's been advanced since the beginning. Her body has just caught up with her. I guess if you think about it, this was the way it was always meant to be. Otherwise, why would she have had powers well before any other young magician in history?"

That made sense, more than most things Liv knew to be true. But it wasn't what she wanted to hear. Liv wanted someone to say that what had happened to Sophia was an injustice. That it was wrong. That it should be fixed. She could fight arguments like that, but knowing what had happened to Sophia was right made anything that would come next difficult.

"It's going to be okay," Bermuda said, an odd thoughtfulness in her voice and radiating from her eyes that Liv wasn't accustomed to seeing from the giantess.

Still, she nodded as she watched her and the other two giants retreat into the house.

When Liv couldn't ignore her sister standing at her back or the darkening cloud hanging over her head anymore, she finally straightened. Turned. Looked at the little girl who wasn't so little anymore.

"You grew up," Liv said, choking on the three short words.

"In one hour," Sophia agreed, coughing on her own words.

"I knew that things were changing—"

"But not so fast," Sophia said, completing her sentence.

"Does this mean you're leaving?" Liv asked, glancing at the still unbroken egg.

"Not yet," Sophia answered. She was wearing black pants and an armored top. Strangely, for the first time ever, her outfit resembled Liv's, although it had flair. In total Sophia fashion, her clothes had that extra bit of flair that made her appear edgy and beautifully timeless.

After watching Liv study her clothes for a moment, Sophia glanced down. "I thought this was more practical than a dress, although I'm not giving those up permanently yet. I just wanted to cover all the bits and boobs."

Liv couldn't believe how grown up her sister sounded. However, she reminded herself that she'd always sounded grown up. It was just that her squeaky voice contradicted that impression much of the time.

"Yes, you have two boobs now," Liv said, averting her eyes from Sophia's chest.

Her sister giggled. "Do they make things harder?"

"They make it different," Liv stated. "But being a girl... well, a woman, is amazing. You just have to embrace who you are."

Sophia took a step forward. "That's hard when everything is changing so fast."

Liv took a step forward too. "Yes, but you're too wonderful to not love who you're becoming, even if it's not following the timeline we expected."

"Are you mad?" Sophia asked when she was only a couple of feet from Liv.

Now that she was close, Liv was able to see the intricacies of her face. Gone were the baby cheeks and childlike features. As if Liv hadn't suspected this would be the case, Sophia looked much like their mother, Guinevere Beaufont. She was absolutely gorgeous. Unlike before, her features had smoothed out. Her cheekbones were prominent. Her lips full. Her eyes were almond-shaped, and her nose as beautifully round as a button.

"Soph, how could I be mad?" Liv asked, and meant it. "You can't control this. And even if you could, would you want to stop it?"

Her sister shook her head.

"All I ever wanted for you was a life that makes you happy," Liv stated. "I might worry. I might miss you. I might, as in this moment right now, wish things had happened differently. But I'm confident that in the future, I'll be absolutely grateful that things happened exactly as they did. Sophia Beaufont, whatever you do is going to change the world for the better. You're going to be the most incredible dragon rider in history, and I'm grateful that I can watch your evolution."

When her little sister rushed to Liv, she was taken aback by actually how little she *wasn't*. The strength of Sophia's embrace nearly knocked Liv off-balance, but she recovered, holding her sister tight and realizing that she was exactly her height now.

Liv released several tears and so did Sophia, their sobs communicating both the fear and the excitement of the future for both of them.

When the storm broke overhead, Liv wasn't sad when rain began to drench them. Showers might flood or drown, but they did so much more. Liv realized the rains brought what the earth needed to refresh itself and grow anew.

CHAPTER EIGHT

L iv rushed into the House of Fourteen with her hood covering her head, drenched from the short walk from the portal. That was why, when she shook off the rain-drenched cape, she thought she'd entered through the wrong palm-reading shop. This had happened a few times before. She popped her head out the door, checking to see that it was the right one. It was.

In the past, when she didn't recognize the House, it was because a major change had happened. When she'd revealed the truth about the Mortal Seven, the House's foyer had expanded. When the first of the Mortal Seven, John Carraway, had entered the House, the statues of the original fourteen had appeared, lining the main hallway. But now... This didn't make any sense.

The usually large entryway with gold walls and high ceilings appeared wrecked, like a condemned house. The floor was broken and dirty. The hallway was short and narrow, with many holes in the wall. And worst of all, there was a horrid smell, like there was something that had been dead for a long time under the floorboards.

Liv covered her nose, squinting in the darkness.

"Well, this can't be good," Plato said, having materialized by her side.

"What does this mean?" Liv asked, finding it difficult to talk without inhaling in the polluted air.

"Maybe someone forgot to make a mortgage payment," Plato offered.

Liv shook her head. "I don't think so. I just don't get it. I killed Kayla. She's gone."

"It appears you have more enemies to get rid of," Plato stated.

Liv took a careful step forward, unable to make out her path. A chilly breeze shot through the hall as she entered. The walls that were usually dazzling with the language of the founders were dark and covered in something.

"What is that?" Liv asked, trying to get a closer look.

"I wouldn't do that," Plato warned her.

Liv jumped back a moment later, realizing why he'd warned her. "Blood? The walls are covered in blood?"

"And I don't believe the design appeared by accident," Plato continued.

Liv took a step back but wasn't able to easily get a good view in the cramped space. "Are those symbols?"

Plato nodded. "I think it's the founders' language."

Liv pulled out her mother's ring. The Warrior's ring, actually, that she always kept with her. She had trouble thinking of the piece of jewelry as hers, maybe because all her life, she'd associated it with her mother.

The large central gem glowed brightly as she ran it over

a set of symbols, giving her some much-needed light. However, seeing the dark crimson blood dripping down the walls wasn't a welcoming sight, not like the golden wall that used to be there with symbols that danced under her fingers.

The ring seemed to have trouble interpreting the symbols, unlike before.

"It must be because everything is smearing together," Liv observed, watching as blood from above dripped onto the symbols.

"I wonder if it says, 'red rum,'" Plato suggested.

Liv sighed, rolling her eyes at the lynx. "Really? You're making jokes right now?"

"Well, the joke won't make any sense if I wait until later."

Liv continued to run the ring over the symbols, wishing it would interpret at least one of them. However, when she'd made it down the short hallway, she realized it was useless. Whatever the House was trying to tell her was lost.

A chill ran down Liv's back when she turned to face the way she'd come. She didn't understand. All of the Councilors and Warriors had been tested with a lie detector, and they had all passed. However, it appeared there was still someone or something deceptive in the House.

Whatever was going on, it wasn't good. No, actually, it was horrible.

Maybe worse than when Adler had ruled, brainwashing mortals and murdering anyone who got in his way. Liv didn't want to think about what could be worse than that, though.

"Ummm, you might want to see this," Plato said behind her.

Liv was certain that based on the tense tone of his voice, she *didn't* want to see whatever he was referring to. She took a deep breath and turned to face the next room. Surprisingly, it wasn't much different than usual.

The large door that led to the residential wing was exactly the same. To her relief, the Door of Reflection, across from it, was also the same as she remembered. And the space between the doors was just a blank, undescriptive wall.

Liv's hand flew to her mouth as the implications became clear. "The Black Void. It's gone!"

CHAPTER NINE

S winging around, Liv frantically searched, thinking
maybe the Black Void was still there somewhere.
Maybe she'd simply missed it. A quick glance around told
her she hadn't.

"What could this mean?" Liv asked, her breath hitching
in her throat.

"Remember the way the Black Void always made you
feel?" Plato asked.

"How could I ever forget?" Liv answered. "It felt like
impending death. Doom. Despair. Greed. Hatred."

"And how do you feel when you look at the entryway
now?" Plato asked.

"I-I-it feels like the Black Void exploded," Liv said, and
realized that was it.

"Again, I don't think this could be good," Plato stated.

"But what could be causing this?" Liv asked.

"Unfortunately, I think we'll find out very soon." He
indicated the Door of Reflection.

Liv tensed. Never before had she so badly not wanted

to step through the reflective surface that showed her her worst fears. She was certain that whatever she saw would traumatize her for life. Still, she hadn't backed down from facing her fears yet, and she wasn't going to start now. If the House was in trouble, she was going to save it—whatever it took.

"Wish me luck," she said over her shoulder to Plato.

He sighed. "I think you're going to need more than luck."

"Thanks," Liv said dully, stepping through the Door of Reflection.

Blackness encircled Liv. She stood on a hilltop, looking down at the city she called home. Los Angeles lay in ruins. For miles, fires raged, smoke wafted through the air, and sirens blared. The city was past saving. Screams all around Liv told her that most were in danger. She couldn't get to them all. She couldn't save her city, and deep in her soul, she knew if Los Angeles looked this way, many other cities across the world did too.

The world was on fire, and magic was to blame.

Something had gone very, very wrong.

---

As Liv had expected, the images she's seen in the Door of Reflection felt as if they would be trapped in her forever. When she stepped into the Chamber of the Tree, she couldn't shake the ruins she'd seen in her waking dream. At her core, she felt raw, like she'd already grieved for the end of the world as she knew it.

The faces of the Warriors and Councilors told Liv that

they'd seen the ruined entryway too. Everyone stared at her with somber eyes, many blinking as if in a daze. Jude paced in the center of the room as he panted like he was suffering from heat exhaustion. The black crow was nowhere to be found, which made the foreboding in Liv's chest worsen.

John bolted upright at the sight of her. "Did you see? It's gone."

Liv gulped. "I know, and the main hallway…"

"What are you talking about?" Bianca asked John. "Why do you keep saying something is gone?"

"The Black Void," Liv answered, looking at her friend. "The others can't see it, remember? They didn't know it was there, and now it's gone."

He nodded, took a seat, and picked up Pickles.

"Will you explain what you're talking about?" Lorenzo asked, looking down the bench at John, Ireland, and Cassie. The Mortal Seven glanced at Liv, apprehension on their faces.

"There is…well, there *was* this large swirling blackness that I call the Black Void," Liv began to explain.

"Because that is what it looks like," John added.

"Yes," Liv affirmed. "But also, that name just fit."

"Because it's correct," Clark said, furiously turning the pages of the *Forgotten Archives*, which he carried with him everywhere he went. He was studying the book from cover to cover, which would pretty much take most of his life to do properly. "I found a mention of the Black Void in here. It's a refuge in the House of Fourteen that only the founders could use if they needed a protective place. In the early days, they worried that other magical races wouldn't accept them. At one point, they thought there might be a war and they'd have to take shelter."

"What happened?" Stefan asked. He knew better than most that the history they all understood was different from what had actually transpired. It had been altered when the mortals' understanding of magic had been erased.

"I'm not sure," Clark answered. "All I know is that only founder families can see it, and only those connected to mortals, or who are actually founders, or are drawn there by one."

Well, that explained why Clark couldn't see it although Liv could, and it explained why the Takahashi brothers couldn't see it either. Liv had been connected to John since the beginning. Well, not when she was a child, but she'd sensed it even then.

"So this Black Void disappeared," Hester said speculatively. "What does that mean? And what does it mean that the hallway has been destroyed?"

"Could one of the founders be back?" Raina asked.

Liv looked at Stefan, more for support than anything. He nodded at her, filling her with a confidence that few could give her. His pure blue eyes were full of conviction.

"I don't think any of us can speculate about what this could mean," Liv said. "I think we all need to be on guard. The display in the hallway means that a new evil is out there. The best thing we can do is find the rest of the Mortal Seven. That is how we'll protect this organization."

Liv was surprised by her own words, but they felt strangely right to her.

"I think Liv is right," Trudy DeVries said, stepping

forward. "They will protect us, and we will protect them. Assembling the House as it was is the first priority."

"Okay, so we go after the Mortal Seven," Haro said, looking down at his tablet. "There are four more families."

"It will take too long for me to recover them on my own," Liv said, again surprised by her words but sensing their truth. "The other Warriors should be assigned to help, but I have to teach them the chimera song first. That's the only way to unlock them."

"Okay," Raina said. "Do you know where to look?"

Liv pulled a piece of parchment from her pocket. "Yes, I got the list from…"

She let the sentence die away before she told anyone that Mortimer, the head of the brownies, had told her where the rest of the Mortal Seven were located.

"Okay," Hester said, making the list fly to her fingers. "So we assign this to three of the Warriors. But then—"

Liv's phone rang in her pocket although it was on silent. She gave the council an apologetic look as she retrieved the phone. "Sorry," she said, holding the phone up to her ear.

"Yes," she replied.

The voice on the other end of her phone was urgent, frustrated, and gave her little room to argue.

"Okay," she said when granted a moment to speak. "I'll be there."

When she clicked off the phone, she gave the Council another apologetic look. "Sorry. I'm here, but I have to go very soon."

"Yes, to go and recover one of the Mortal Seven," Raina said.

Liv backed away for the door. "Actually, no. You all will have to recover the rest of the Mortal Seven on your own." Her heart was beating faster than she remembered it ever doing. Nothing was right in her world. Sophia had changed in an hour. The House was in disrepair. And now this.

Stefan turned to her with a look which gave her hope that things could be right again.

She looked him straight in the eyes, giving him a confident nod. "It's fine."

"It can't be if you're leaving, Liv," Clark said, looking like he was about to spring out of his chair.

"No, it's not, Clark. But it will be. I promise," Liv stated. "The Father of Time has gone missing. I'll return when I can."

# CHAPTER TEN

Subner hadn't given Liv much information. He'd simply said that Papa Creola was missing and to get to the Fantastical Armory pronto.

Liv couldn't fathom how the most powerful entity on Earth could have gone missing. She knew that something had been after Papa Creola lately, but she'd never considered the possibility that it could actually take him.

She suddenly felt like she was a small child again as she rushed down Roya Lane, swerving to avoid elves selling sage and gnomes making deals in the street. She remembered waking in the middle of the night and getting out of bed for no apparent reason when she was six years old.

Her little feet had soundlessly carried her to the study, where her father was pacing in front of the fireplace, his hands clenching the back of his head. She watched for a long moment as stress dripped from his features. His footsteps grew heavier with each lap across the study. Little Liv knew something was wrong with her father. She'd never seen him so worried, and yet, she didn't know what to do. If he knew she was out of bed, he might be mad. She might make him even more upset. She couldn't bear that thought.

Before she could retreat or speak up, the phone rang. Theodore Beaufont rushed to the desk and picked it up.

"Hello," he said, his tone urgent.

He was silent for a moment, his eyes narrowed.

"She's still missing?" he asked over the telephone. "And no one has seen her? It's not like Guinevere to be gone this long."

A sob she couldn't muffle escaped Liv's mouth. Her father looked up then, panic on his face.

"Olivia," her father said, his voice cracking on her name. "Oh, no. You heard?"

Liv took a step backward, shaking her head, but not in answer to her father's question. Not until that moment had she considered that something bad could happen to her parents. They were always there. Always strong. The foundation of her world.

It was at that young age that Liv had realized for the first time ever that as incredible as her mother was, she was vulnerable. She could go missing. She could disappear forever.

Suddenly, as she rushed to the Fantastical Armory, Liv felt like that small, fragile child again. She'd never considered that something could happen to Papa Creola, and yet, he was missing. What would happen to the world without him? What would happen to time? The implications of losing someone who balanced so much were startling.

Thankfully, Guinevere had shown up the next morning. Her face had been cut in several places and her clothes were badly ripped, but she was alive. Apparently, she'd encountered a group of rogue magicians who didn't want to conform to the laws of the House since it kept them from running scams on mortals.

Liv nearly gasped at the memory as it played in her head. She'd forgotten the last part. The group her mother had been unable to stop, the one that had nearly killed her, was called the Renegades.

It was hard for Liv to believe that the group that she, John, and Alicia had been tracking was the same one that had nearly taken her mother out all those years ago. Alicia had put a tracker on Chloe, John's ex-wife, and the three of them were hopeful she'd lead them to the source of the rebel group. But that was going to have to wait. Liv's total focus was on Papa Creola. She hoped that much like her mother, he showed back up. If not, she'd do everything possible to find him.

She'd made a promise to the council and she fully intended to keep it. Liv would get Papa Creola back, whatever it took.

---

Ironically, Subner was pacing the shop with his hand clenching the back of his head when Liv entered the shop.

He glanced up, startled by the sight of her. "It took you long enough."

Normally, she would have shot a snappy comeback at him, but this wasn't the time.

"What's happened?" Liv asked, searching the shop for

clues. It was as pristine as ever, all the cases polished, and the weapons within them sparkling.

"I don't know," Subner answered, continuing to pace.

Liv lowered her chin, trying to keep her frustration at bay. It was a typical for Subner or Papa Creola to give her little information on a case, but in this instance, it felt utterly insulting.

"What do you mean, you don't know?" Liv asked. "How do you know he's missing?"

Subner halted, hesitation dancing in his eyes. "There is a unique magic that bonds me to Papa Creola. It's hard to explain, but I know what he's feeling and thinking and what happens to him, although not the specifics."

"So you know he's missing because you feel it?" Liv asked.

He nodded. "And he hasn't returned any of my calls, which never happens."

Liv gave him a skeptical glare.

"Well, and yes, I know he's in danger," Subner went on. "But that's the feeling I've been getting for a while. However, it intensified recently. I don't know what's happened to him. I don't even know where to tell you to start looking, but I do know that if you don't find him, everything in this world hangs in the balance."

Liv sucked in a breath. "Okay. I'll find him."

She turned, heading for the door.

"Oh, and Liv?" Subner called.

She swung around to face the gnome. "What?"

He snapped his fingers, and a small package appeared in his hands. "Papa asked me to give this to you should anything ever happen to him."

Liv took a cautionary step forward. "What is it?"

He handed it to her. "I'm not sure. He just said that if something ever happened to him, I needed to hand it off to you and that you weren't to open it until all other possibilities of rescuing him were lost."

Liv took it. "So you know what he's feeling and thinking and lots of other things, but not what's in the small package he gave you with an ominous message regarding his potential demise?"

Subner sighed and relented. "Okay, although I don't know entirely what it is, I sense that it is something of great power. If Papa wanted you to have it in his absence, I'm guessing it's a piece of him."

Liv grimaced. "Eww, like a toe or something?"

Subner rolled his small eyes. "No, like part of his power. In the past, when he's feared for himself, he's sealed some of his magic away in case it would be needed to rescue him or fix the world. I can't tell you that the same is true this time, but I'm guessing it is."

"And I'm not to open it unless there are no other options?" Liv asked, feeling like this was all an odd setup.

Subner nodded. "It's a last resort, which is what makes me think whatever it is has incredible power. It could have the potential to burn out your magic, or to age you, or to end your life entirely."

Liv eyed the package with a lot less interest, holding it away from her.

"Hopefully you won't need it," Subner offered.

"Yeah, I sort of like my magic. Well, and my life," she said, slipping the package into her cape.

"But Papa Creola wouldn't have made you one of his

unless he knew you had what it took in the worst-case scenario," Subner stated. "He knows that if necessary, you'll risk it all to preserve the greater good."

Liv nodded, feeling heavy and hoping Papa Creola had put his faith in the right person.

## CHAPTER ELEVEN

L iv's feet carried her without her consent. They seemed to know exactly where she needed to go next. She was unsurprised when she arrived at the head office for the brownies on autopilot.

Pricilla greeted her warmly when she entered the main area.

Ticker, on the other hand, ran over, arms waving wildly over his head, ears flapping. "Biv Leaufont! Biv Leaufont!"

Liv happily picked up the little brownie, hugging him tightly. She hadn't realized how much she'd missed him until then. It could have also been the foreboding of doom that seemed to be hovering over her related to the House and Papa Creola. She had to admit that she needed a hug much more than usual.

She gave Ticker to his mother, who looked ready to burst with another baby. "I'm sorry. I'd like to take more time to visit, but I need to talk to Mortimer pronto."

Pricilla seemed to understand, even if Ticker wanted more time with her. He wailed in his mother's arms.

Liv strode into Mortimer's office, not offering the same formalities as usual. "Mort, I need help. It's Papa Creola."

The head official for the brownies looked up. "What's wrong, Warrior Beaufont for the House of Fourteen?"

Maybe it was the hug from Ticker that had softened her, or the accumulation of all the other feelings rising to the surface, but for some reason, Liv felt tender, like she might cry. She knew that emotion couldn't always be shrugged off.

She remembered what her mother had once told her when she cried. "The ability to feel doesn't make you weak. If anything, it means that life is preparing you for something that most aren't strong enough to handle."

Liv let her mother's words wash over her as she opened her mouth to speak. "It's Papa Creola. He's…well, I don't know, actually. I was hoping you could tell me. He's gone missing, but we don't know where to look."

Mortimer's eyes widened in shock. Liv had never seen the brownie appear so fearful. "I knew this day would come, but I didn't think it would come yet."

"Can you help?" Liv asked.

The brownie went straight to work, typing on his keyboard. "I can try."

Liv didn't know what that meant and worried it wouldn't be enough, but then he added. "I've called every brownie off their jobs and asked them to look for Papa Creola," he stated with confidence. "If he's out there, one of mine will find him."

"But what about—"

Mortimer held up a tiny hand, pausing her. "Yes, mortals' homes will suffer. Yes, my main objective will fail.

But if anything happens to Papa Creola, it will matter very little. He is the priority."

Liv bowed, grateful for the brownies' help. "Will you let me know when you hear something?"

He nodded. "The very second I do. In the meantime, do what you do best: keep this world safe."

Liv nodded back at him. "Thank you. I'll do my best."

# CHAPTER TWELVE

L iv felt like she should be doing something. Anything but pacing in John's electronics repair shop. But strangely, when she craved a task, there was nothing to be done. Before, she would have been grateful for the break, but things had changed drastically.

Papa Creola was missing, and more than anything Liv wanted to do something to help find him. But that was Mortimer's job now. All she could do was wait, which was the worst job ever.

The other Warriors had all gone off to find the rest of the Mortal Seven. Alicia had repaired every electronic device that had entered the shop. And weirdly, there were no other pressing cases.

Liv felt like Subner and her father as she paced the shop, trying to expel the nervous energy bounding out of her chest.

When the door chimed as it opened, she actually jumped like a spooked cat whose adrenal gland was working overtime.

John gave her a careful expression as he entered. "Are you okay? What about Papa Creola? Is *he* okay?"

She shook her head as Alicia strode in behind him. "Nothing yet. I'm just waiting to get information."

"Okay, well, now might not be the best time for this, but Alicia has found the location of the Renegades," John explained, referring to the rebel group that Chloe, his ex-wife, was a part of.

Liv darted over, eyeing the scientist. "Where is it? Do you have it on you? Give it to me now! I'll go immediately."

Alicia pulled out a tablet. "Yes, I know the location. I was able to track Chloe and find where she spends most of her time. That has to be the location of the Renegades. It's a warehouse, and if the heat signatures I've been monitoring are correct, there are a few dozen magicians in there."

"Give it to me," Liv said, surprised to find herself snapping her fingers.

John held up a hand. "Fighting the Renegades is important, but Papa Creola is more so. Shouldn't you keep your focus free in case something arises?"

Since he'd taken on his role as a Mortal Seven, he'd exhibited new confidence enhanced by age-old wisdom. It suited him, but just then, Liv didn't need his sage advice.

"No, I need to be on a case," she argued. "The wait is excruciating, and if anything comes in about Papa Creola, I'll drop everything. He is the priority. However, I have a feeling that finding him won't be easy. Whoever wanted him is powerful, or they wouldn't be able to track him down and abduct him or whatever they've done to the little guy. And I suspect they'll have him extremely well-guarded, making it harder to find him. In the meantime, I need a case. I need to go after the Renegades."

"Okay, then my other concern is that this should go through the council," John stated.

"That will just delay things," Liv countered. "If they got the case, who would they assign it to?"

"Well, you're the only free Warrior at the moment since the others are tracking down the rest of the Mortal Seven," John answered. "So you, of course."

"Exactly!" Liv stated.

"But if my memory of the Renegades is correct, they are a very powerful group," John said. "I know you're strong and the best we have, but I'm not sure you should be going on this case alone. Alicia says there are a few dozen magicians in there."

Liv distinctly remembered the morning her mother came home after battling the Renegades. She'd never seen her so bruised and beaten up. "I can do it. I really *need* to do it."

John let out a long breath. "Liv, I know you're antsy to get your mind off things, but—"

"I faced down Sid Encore, and he's one of the Renegades," Liv argued.

"If I remember correctly, you did that with Stefan," he stated.

This was actually the job of a Councilor, and John did it well. He provided objectivity when Liv's Warrior spirit was thirsty for vengeance.

She closed her eyes for a half-beat, trying to think clearly.

"What if I go with her?" Alicia offered.

"What?" John spun to face the scientist, surprise on his face.

"Liv and I work well together," Alicia answered. "We did a great job in Venice, and I've got a ton of magic tech I've been wanting to test. And I'm the perfect person to go with Liv because I've been watching this location and have some ideas about the security."

"But you're not trained for combat," John declared.

"Yes, but I don't have to be," Alicia argued. "I can use my devices. Those should get us into the warehouse and keep us undetected until Liv rounds up all the scoundrels."

John thought about it for a moment. "I still don't know."

"Look," Liv began, "I have to do this. Not just because I desperately need a case, but also because this group eluded my mom. I owe it to her memory to take them down once and for all."

"Okay," John acquiesced. "But if Chloe sees you two, she'll recognize you from the shop. You don't just need to get in there, but also go unnoticed until you can take down the leader. That's how all organizations fall."

Liv had never been so proud of her friend. He thought strategically, as if he was born to be a Councilor for the House of Fourteen—which he literally had been.

Liv looked at Alicia speculatively. "I've got a hat. Will that work?"

She laughed. "I'm not sure that's enough. And John is right. From everything I can tell, the warehouse is full of magicians. That's all I know, so it would be good if we can have some time in there before we shut them down."

Disguises weren't Liv's thing. They were…

As if summoned by her thoughts, Sophia entered the

shop, looking mature and beautiful and very much like her mother. Liv still wasn't used to seeing the grown-up Sophia. She wasn't sure how long it would take her to get used to the change. And then she realized one very important thing: she'd forgotten to tell John.

The shop owner gave Sophia a welcoming smile. "Hello, young lady. How can I help you today?"

Even though she'd aged several years, that trademark giggle still sounded like the one Sophia'd had when she was smaller. "John, it's me. Sophia."

He spun to face Liv as if she'd tell him it was all a practical joke.

She nodded. "It's true. Apparently, her body did some rapid aging to help her to catch up with Charles."

"You mean, her dragon?" Alicia asked.

"Yes," Liv answered.

"Oh, wow," John said, sliding his hand over his head. "This is… Well, you look… You're simply…"

"Beautiful," Alicia said, helping him out.

"And as someone who has gone back on the age scale, I know how weird it is for others to see you afterward," John said to Sophia. "I'm therefore sorry if I'm looking at you funny. I just can't get over that the little girl I met recently appears all grown up suddenly."

"Me either," Liv said dully.

Sophia smiled at her. "On the bright side, we can share clothes now."

"You won't want anything in my closet. It's all black and boring," Liv said, but then a thought occurred to her. "But hey, we could use your help with disguises, if you're up for it."

# CHAPTER THIRTEEN

"My nose feels different," Liv said, pressing her finger against one nostril and blowing out a breath.

"That's because it is," Sophia stated, slapping her hand away. "Don't mess with it until it's set."

Liv gawked at her. "Like it's wet paint?"

"Sort of," Sophia answered.

"I get that it's different-looking, but I can't breathe as well," she explained to her little sister.

"Well, that's because Rocky, the person I gave you as a disguise, has a deviated septum," Sophia informed, turning her attention to Alicia.

"Do you come up with a whole backstory for these disguises you make up?" Liv asked.

Sophia nodded, morphing Alicia's dark brown hair into a white bun on the top of her head. Her usually smooth skin was suddenly lined with wrinkles, making her appear old. "Yes, disguises work best if you have character depth. Like for instance, Rocky used to be a bouncer at a club, which was how he broke his nose. He's been trying to find a good healer to fix it, but he doesn't trust that brand of magic since he lost a friend who went to get a simple operation done."

"Wow, you've written a whole book about this Rocky guy." Liv looked in the mirror, grimacing at her image. Not only did the crooked nose make her appear unattractive, but Rocky also had quite a few scars on his face and head that sectioned off his short black hair and whiskers. "This guy saw quite a few fights as a bouncer."

"Well, yeah. That's because he worked at one of the roughest magician bars," Sophia answered. "The one on the east side that serves beer in skulls."

Liv sighed and glanced at John. "They grow up so fast, don't they?"

John laughed. "Literally."

"What's my person's story?" Alicia asked, sidling up next to Liv to gaze at her image in the mirror.

"You're Louise. You work at the library during the day, but at night, you're a spy for the Renegades, trying to get information about the House," Sophia stated. "You have three cats named Whiskers, Fluffy, and Paws."

"You lack imagination when it comes to names," Liv said to Alicia.

"How long will their disguises last?" John asked, worry coating his features.

"For a few hours, or until they remove them using magic," Sophia stated.

"That should be enough time," Liv said, trying to fasten Bellator around her midsection but finding that her gut was too large for the belt. "Ummm, did you have to make me so rotund?"

"Well, I thought the extra weight might come in handy since Alicia said you'd be in charge of combat and she'd be running the tech portion," Sophia explained, twirling her finger and pointing at Liv. A belt and sheath appeared on her waist. "Try that and see if it works."

Liv slipped Bellator into the sheath and relaxed, feeling better now that she had her sword at her side. "I guess I'm going to have to magick some clothes onto me when I shift to myself."

"Do you feel comfortable enough to do that?" Sophia asked.

Liv nodded. "I'm no Sophia Beaufont when it comes to disguises, but I can manage simple wardrobe changes."

Alicia reached into a box on the counter and retrieved several devices. "I think I have enough stuff to get us in there and serve as a distraction."

Liv looked around, trying to figure out if she was forgetting anything. "Then I think we're ready to go. John, will you stay with Sophia? Although she looks old enough to drive, she's still nine years old."

He nodded, apprehension heavy in his eyes. "Yes, Pickles and I will take good care of her. But I need you two to be extra careful. The Renegades are lethal."

Liv smiled victoriously. "Which is why we're going to take them down."

CHAPTER FOURTEEN

The warehouse was located in an industrial area that had minimal traffic. Liv searched the perimeter while Alicia studied a device in her hands. So far, only a few magicians had gone into the building in the last twenty minutes, and none had left. All of them had that shifty look about them, same as Chloe.

"There are about two dozen people in the headquarters," Alicia informed her. "However, I don't think all of them are magicians."

"Well, the gnomes and elves aren't especially fond of the House right now either," Liv explained. "I could see them joining up with the Renegades."

Alicia shook her head. "Gnomes make sense, but these definitely aren't elves. They are too small."

She showed her the screen that displayed the heat signatures of everyone in the building. Liv made out many different red and orange blobs that could easily belong to magicians, but she understood immediately what Alicia meant. There were a few blobs that were too small to belong to full-grown adult magicians.

"Could they be children?" Liv asked.

Alicia squinted at the screen. "I'm not sure. The layout of the building does seem like a compound. It could be communal, with several families living in it."

Liv sighed. She hadn't factored children in. That would make things more complicated. The Renegades were bad magicians who abused their magic and took advantage of mortals and others. However, their children were innocent and shouldn't be punished along with their parents.

"Okay, this is exactly why we need to get in there undetected," Liv said, staring at the entrance. "Once we are inside, we can get more information."

Alicia held up a simple-looking card. "I have exactly what we need to get in."

"Is that a credit card?" Liv asked, wondering if the scientist was going to bribe her way into the warehouse.

She shook her head. "No, it's a universal keycard. Before, when I was stalking...I mean, watching Chloe, I noticed she had a card that allowed her entrance into the building. I created this, and it should work."

Liv smiled at her friend. "I realize that you were stalking...I mean, watching Chloe because I asked you to, but you didn't by chance have a more personal interest in keeping tabs on the evil magician, did you?"

"Well, it definitely wasn't so I could find out where hussy buys her dresses," Alicia answered at once and then softened. "And yes, I might have been curious about this magician who was once married to John."

Liv nodded. "That hussy wears heels that would end me

in a second and swooping necklines like she doesn't want any man staring her straight in the eye ever, but I think it's normal to be curious about your guy's ex-wife."

Alicia's face blossomed red. "I don't really think he's my guy. I mean, we haven't discussed it or anything."

"But you spend every moment together when he's not at the House and you adore each other, right?" Liv questioned.

If possible, the crimson color of Alicia's face deepened, contrasting with her white hair. "So you've noticed."

"Astronauts in space have noticed," Liv stated. "I couldn't be happier for you two. And I realize that John is going through a lot of changes lately and may be trying to take things slow, afraid he'll mess it up. That's the only reason. It has nothing to do with that witch he used to be married to."

Alicia nodded and stared at the ground. "I know. It's just so weird to think of him with her. He's so loving and pure, and she's such a manipulative—"

"Bitch," Liv supplied. "That's the word you're looking for, and the one that fits best. But remember, John always tries to see the best in people. As a Mortal Seven, he saw Chloe's magic, which would have been captivating to him before he knew the truth about himself. Even so, Chloe is corrupt from the inside. I believe she took advantage of John. Probably felt that her powers increased when she was around him and used him for that. Then, when she had gained enough power, she dumped him, telling him he'd never understand her world."

Alicia laughed, rubbing her hands together with a

vengeance. "And ironically, he's now part of what will destroy her defunct world."

Liv patted her friend on the shoulder. "For a librarian, you sort of scare me."

Shooting her a sly grin, Alicia said, "Well, I'd rather be in this form for this mission than be a chicken."

"Yeah, I'm grateful I don't have to carry you this time," Liv agreed.

Holding open the bag full of devices, Alicia smiled. "Oh, I plan to be way more helpful than when I was a dumb chicken. I'm going to help you to take these lawbreakers down."

Liv nodded, then returned her gaze to the warehouse full of Renegades. "Yes, once and for all, the Renegades are about to meet their end."

## CHAPTER FIFTEEN

"Just act natural," Alicia said, striding next to Liv across the parking lot surrounding the warehouse.

"Easy for you to say," Liv countered, still put off by how deep her voice was. She sounded like Rory. "You don't have a beer belly and whistle when you breathe."

"That's true," Alicia stated. "But Louise has an underbite, and it keeps making me bite my tongue when I talk."

"I have an easy solution for that," Liv offered, scanning the outside of the building and noting many security cameras.

"Fine," Alicia answered. "I'll be quiet. And don't worry about those. I'll have them jammed in just a second."

Liv noticed a small clicker in Alicia's bony fingers. She pointed it in the direction of the closest camera and clicked once, then did it three more times as she pointed the device at the other cameras.

"Are they..." Liv dared to ask.

"They are on a loop from two minutes earlier," Alicia stated. "Well before we strolled into view."

"I'm sure I'll say this many, many more times in the next hour, but you're a genius." Liv strode up to the door, her eyes sliding to the card reader beside it. She casually glanced over her shoulder, as if checking that she'd turned her headlights off as Alicia held the universal keycard under the reader. It beeped once, allowing them entry.

Letting out a long breath, Liv yanked open the door, trying to remember Rocky's persona. As Sophia needed it to make the disguise more realistic, Liv needed it to convince other people that she was Rocky.

They entered a small room with a guard who was picking his teeth with a chipped blade. He straightened, looking them over. "Who you?"

Liv paid him little notice, her eyes darting to the door on the other side. "We're Renegades. What do you think?"

"I don't recognize you," the guard said, scanning them with his beady eyes.

"And I don't recognize you," Alicia said, her voice high-pitched and hands pressed to her stomach like she was cold.

"I'm going to need to see what's in your bag," the guard said, pointing to Alicia. Then he looked at Liv. "And you're going to need a good pat-down, although you can be certain I won't enjoy doing it."

Before Liv could respond, Alicia stepped forward. "We are from the other office, and we have business with your boss."

"My boss?" the guard said, a sly grin on his face like he'd caught them.

Liv's hand slid to Bellator.

"Yes, Lucian, of course," Alicia stated confidently. "And in case you're wondering, it's the office in New York."

"Oh, well," the guard said, deflating slightly. "I'm still going to need to pat this one down. I'll let your bag go, though. My mom always told me it was impolite to look in a woman's purse."

Alicia nodded, her chin held high. "He's only got the goods Lucian sent him to retrieve."

Liv had no idea who Lucian was or how Alicia knew anything about this person. However, when her friend gave her an encouraging nod, Liv simply held up her hands, allowing the guard to search her. He pulled out Bellator at once, his eyes running hungrily over the blade.

"Wow, this is a prize your office got?" the guard asked.

Liv snatched the sword back. "Yes, and it isn't for you."

The guard snapped back from the force of her grab. She hadn't realized how strong she was. That was going to make things fun. "Right. Right you are. Lucian will be happy with such a prize. Your 'chauns are having way more luck than ours. I think we got a defunct bunch."

"Can we go now?" Alicia asked, impatience heavy in her tone like the library was closing soon and she was antsy to get home to her cats.

The guard nodded, suddenly seeming eager to help. "Go on in. Lucian is straight through the hallway, up the stairs, and in the office on the right."

Liv grunted in reply, following Alicia through the door. Once they were through, Liv waited to ensure they were alone. The hallway was long, about one hundred yards, with multiple doors on either side. At the far end was a set of stairs. Behind the doors, a ruckus was emanating from the various rooms. Overhead were lights that swung like there was a draft wafting through the rafters, and in the air was the smell of sweat and dirt.

"How?" Liv asked simply.

Alicia kept her chin high as they sped down the long hallway. She tapped the side of her face. "I'm wearing a contact lens that allows me to see thoughts."

Liv huffed. "Okay, you could have told me that before we came in here."

Alicia released a sly grin. "I like surprising you sometimes. You get to do this stuff all the time. Not me, though."

"So you read his thoughts?" Liv asked, indicating the door they'd just come through.

"Well, I have to ask a specific question and wait for them to answer it in their head," Alicia explained in a whisper. "So I supplied the information I wanted him to respond to. He then thought of his boss, Lucian, and I was able to pretend."

The noise coming from the various rooms they passed was so loud that Liv thought it unlikely anyone could hear them. She kept hearing Alicia click the device that was messing with the cameras, so hopefully, they were still safe.

"So who are the 'chauns?" Liv asked. "And now there's a New York office?"

"I'm not sure," Alicia answered. "It appears so, but I got the impression from the guard's thoughts that they are small and ineffective."

"Again, you're a genius," Liv said, impressed that Alicia had invented magic tech that allowed her to read thoughts.

When they got to the staircase, Liv and Alicia tried to go up together but rammed into each other, thanks to

Rocky's wide shoulders. She held out her arms. "Ladies first."

Alicia nodded appreciatively. "Are you ready for this?"

Liv thought of her mother's battered face when she'd returned that fearful night. "Yes. I've been waiting for this most of my life."

# CHAPTER SIXTEEN

Three doors greeted them when Liv and Alicia reached the top of the stairs. Alicia took out the cameras with a few swift clicks, then pulled out her tablet, scanning for heat signatures in the different rooms.

Soundlessly, she pointed to the door two doors on the left and mouthed the word, "Children."

Liv nodded, not prepared for having small kids in this fight. She'd have to be extra careful and ironically felt awkward in Rocky's body. His long arms knocked into the walls and made her feel less than graceful.

Alicia studied the tablet again. She eyed the door on the right, indicating it with her thumb. "Lucian," she mouthed.

So far, Liv didn't have any bright ideas about how to systematically take down the entire compound of lawbreakers. She had been hoping that by that point, something brilliant would have occurred to her. However, the warehouse had limited entrances and exits. The main area was a long, narrow hallway that would quickly turn into a bottleneck when chaos broke out.

There was no portaling allowed in the building, a quick test told her, which meant, Lucian couldn't easily escape. But it also meant that if she and Alicia were cornered, they couldn't either. And to complicate things even more, there was a room full of children that Liv needed to get out of the building unharmed.

The best she could hope for was to meet with Lucian, find out more information, and then arrest him and any of his goons who didn't get away. The original idea was still true: Take down the leader and the pack will fall. But now Liv had the New York office to think about. Who knew how many Renegade groups were there?

Liv turned back to where the rooms where the children were. Strangely, she heard deep voices coming from behind those doors. It was a collection of muttering that sounded like counting.

"Get back to work!" someone yelled, nearly making Liv jump.

She glanced at Alicia, her eyes wide. The scientist looked down at her tablet and held up a single finger. "One magician in each room," Alicia informed her.

Liv nodded, pressing her ear to one of the doors. That proved to be unnecessary because a moment later, a booming voice shook the floor under her. "Get back to work, or I'm going to get the boss!"

Liv stood back as thundering footsteps echoed across the floor. Shooting an expression of fear at Alicia, she watched as the scientist dug into her bag of tricks. A second later, she handed Liv a small disk.

"Locking device," Alicia whispered.

At once, Liv understood. "You're a genius," she

mouthed, sticking the disk to the first door as Alicia did the same with the other.

They couldn't have the children coming out of the room yet. She'd rescue them all, but not until she had apprehended Lucian. So although she didn't like locking them in the rooms, it was better to contain them with their captors until things were under control.

To her relief, the black disk melted into the door. It would go unnoticed by anyone who didn't know it was in place. There was a gray dot in the center of where the disk was located. Alicia pointed to it. "That's how you unlock it," she whispered.

Liv nodded, grateful she knew the mechanics in case things got crazy.

Turning her attention to the door on the right, she prepared herself for the next phase of the plan. Lucian could have been the leader when her mother tried to take down the Renegades. There was only one way to tell for sure. She took a step forward, her large hand resting just over the doorknob. If Lucian had in fact been the one to rough up her mom, his sentence was going to be a lot longer and more painful.

## CHAPTER SEVENTEEN

"Get in here!" a loud, nasal voice demanded as soon as Liv knocked. She wondered if Lucian had a deviated septum too.

She gave Alicia a speculative glance. "You get him to talk. I'll do the fighting."

Her friend nodded. Liv threw the door open, wanting to make the right entrance. She wished she hadn't because the door swung back, banging into her already broken nose. It had apparently knocked into something on the opposite wall, making it ricochet into her face.

To add insult to injury, the door had fanned the smell of sweat and ash into her face. She suddenly wished that Rocky couldn't smell at all instead of having partially obstructed nostrils.

Lucian was behind a stand-up desk in the middle of the room, an angry scowl on his pale face. Liv saw where the smell of ash came from immediately. In the center of the room was a large metal barrel, and the contents were still smoking like there had recently been a roaring fire.

Liv wanted to point out to the barbarian the safety implications of having a fire in a room with poor ventilation, but she sensed that he wouldn't care much.

Lucian ran his dark brown eyes over her and then Alicia, studying them. Realizing that all Renegades were wannabe badasses, Liv copied his stare. She stood a head taller than the guy.

The short leader of these Renegades had a bald head and a thick beard, making him strangely resemble many of the gnomes Liv knew. That made her think of Papa Creola, pinging her heart with pain. She swallowed it, remembering her current focus.

"Dusty tells me you're with the New York branch," Lucian said, tapping his fingers on his stand-up desk. "Why are you here?"

Alicia took a step forward, clutching her bag to her side. "Why do you think we're here?"

The madman narrowed his eyes at her. "I ask the questions, Missy."

Sticking her pointy chin in the air, Alicia said, "You may call me Miss Louise. And I think you know we're here because Jason sent us. He's struggling with recruitment and needs advice."

Lucian laughed, a sound as disingenuous as the look in his dark eyes. "Jason needs my help, does he? I knew it. When we split, he thought he knew everything and he didn't need me. It was only a matter of time before he would be begging for my expertise."

"And he'd go ask someone else," Liv supplied, needing to know how many more rogue outfits there were.

"But there isn't anyone else," Lucian stated victoriously.

"I'm the only one who has been able to run a successful operation that the House of Stupid hasn't shut down. I might have started small, but thirty years later, we're still doing stuff that goes unnoticed by those pathetic Warriors."

That was all Liv needed to know. This was her man. Well, the man she was going to punish until he cried.

Alicia must have sensed Liv's sudden tension because she stepped forward, cutting off the Warrior's next move, which was to grab Bellator and thrust it through the man's heart. "What would you say is the secret to your success here?"

Lucian shook his head, grimacing at the two of them. "Oh, no. You want information, you better pay up. Dusty tells me you brought me stuff?"

*Noooooo*, Liv yelled in her mind.

Apparently, Alicia's mind-reading lens didn't allow her to read Liv's thoughts because she said, "Yes, we have a sword for you."

Liv simply remained frozen, wondering if she should kill Alicia then or after Lucian.

The person who used to be her friend glanced at her, daring to snap her fingers. "Don't keep Lucian waiting. He doesn't like that," she said, an inflection on the last sentence and emphasis in her eyes.

*Fine*, Liv thought. Alicia had read something in this madman's thoughts that she didn't know about. However, if something happened to Bellator, she was going to hang them both up and bonk their heads together until she was satisfied.

Reluctantly, she pulled Bellator from the sheath at her

waist, noticing how tiny the giant-made sword was in Rocky's hand. It was like a spatula, although it still felt like a menacing weapon that could destroy almost any adversary.

Liv laid the sword in front of the leader of the Renegades and took a step back. Lucian eyed the blade hungrily. "This is most impressive. Your 'chauns were able to recover this?"

Alicia nodded.

The criminal picked up the blade, making Liv twitch with nearly uncontrollable anger.

Beside her, Alicia noticed, giving her a punishing glare.

Thankfully, Lucian didn't register the reaction since his eager eyes were on the blade. "This is of the finest quality. What is it, elven-made?"

"Giant," Liv said too fast.

He cut his eyes at her, a speculative glance in them. "Right, of course. I'm guessing your 'chauns got this off a giant, then?"

"Something like that," Alicia answered.

Lucian let the sword clatter on his desk, seemingly done inspecting it and having no respect for its craftsmanship. "Well, Jason lucked out somehow. Our 'chauns recover all sorts of riches, but it's mostly money. Nothing as unique as this."

"Still, I think there's something we can learn from how you run your operation," Alicia stated.

Lucian opened his mouth, but then caught Liv's eyes resting longingly on Bellator

"Admiring my desk, are you?" he asked, misinterpreting what she was pining for.

"Yeah," Liv answered, nearly choking on the word.

Pridefully, he ran his stumpy fingers over the surface of the desk. "I was having problems with my hips, so my love suggested that I get a stand-up desk. Best investment of other people's money I've made." The scoundrel laughed but quickly stopped when he realized Alicia and Liv weren't laughing with him. They took the hint, bursting into fake chuckles.

"Yeah, those mortals just waste their money on dumb stuff they don't deserve," Alicia said in her high-pitched voice.

Lucian lowered his chin, studying her. "Strangely, that was what I was just thinking."

Alicia laughed again. "That's because it's the right way to think. Mortals should be our slaves, but the House of Ineptitude protects them, especially now that they've allowed them into their ranks."

Lucian smiled, which only made him appear more like a giant gnome. "I can see why Jason sent you to me. You're probably the most competent follower he has. I could definitely use a person who understands these things so well." He then pointed to Rocky. "And I wouldn't mind having muscle like you around. How about you two think about changing locations and working for me?"

Of course, the dog would try and steal Jason's people. That was in line with the Renegades' mentality. They didn't have loyalties, just their own agendas built on a foundation of greed and deceit.

"We might be interested," Alicia told him. "What do you all do here?"

Lucian considered this question for a moment, skepticism came over his features. "The same as you in New York."

"Oh, but we don't do that much," Alicia stated. "We're too busy working on recruitment."

This was apparently the right answer. The mind-reader seemed to be functioning perfectly. Lucian laughed. "Yeah, that sucked up the first few years for me until I recruited my second in command. She takes care of recruitment, which Jason is still struggling with all these years later."

"Yeah, well, we might consider joining you if you filled us in on a bit more of what you do and what we'd be doing for you," Alicia said, and again, Liv wanted to tell her she was a genius. This was exactly what Liv needed information on before she cut the legs out from under this organization. Knowing what the Renegades had been dealing in would help with cleanup, because she was certain that when she brought Lucian down, he'd be unwilling to talk.

"Well, we have the 'chauns, as you know," Lucian began, putting his hands behind his head and leaning back to show off his flexed biceps. "And then there's the nursing homes that we siphon energy off of."

"Nursing homes?" Liv questioned, sounding much angrier than a would-be follower would. She straightened, shaking her head, working to correct her blunder. "That's smart. Why didn't we think of that?"

"Well, yeah," Lucian said. "Once my love realized that our magic increased when we are around mortals, we came up with the idea. No one wants to be around those pesky mortals for long, but nursing homes work well because those are just bags of bones we can use to our benefit."

Liv had to give the Renegades credit; they knew a hell

of a lot more than most magicians. The House had only recently learned that being around mortals increased magical powers since that was the element that they had control over. Magicians, conversely, had wind. Elves had water. Fae had ice. And gnomes fire, and giants earth.

"So you what, go into nursing homes and volunteer?" Alicia asked.

Lucian laughed. "You're a funny one. We go in at night and suck out their energy, usually ending them a bit quicker than they would have without our visits. We think of it as charity. We're putting them out of their misery faster, and as a benefit, all my Renegades are much stronger magicians. They're also unregistered, meaning the House of Incompetence can't shut us down."

Liv had never been a fan of registering magicians, mostly because Adler had led the effort and urged the Warriors to use deadly means to enforce it. Many, like Stefan and Trudy, hadn't complied. However, she could now see the importance of having magicians register. It allowed the House to monitor their magic and stop criminals like these from abusing it. But if it was ever going to be done, it had to be done right. Right now, those who registered were already law-abiding citizens who valued life and magic. Just like with registering cars or anything else, it was those who avoided the law who were most likely to abuse it.

"So you have the 'chauns bringing in your riches, and you take power from mortals," Alicia said, her voice even as she tried to control her temper. "What else do your Renegades do?"

Lucian laughed. "Whatever we like. We don't ask

permission. We don't ask forgiveness either, for that matter. We do whatever we like, with no concern for the law or other races. That is the way it was always meant to be, don't you think?"

Alicia's eyes darted to Liv. She got the message loud and clear. Right now was their chance to make their move. Take Lucian out, then systemically break down his organization of buffoons, finally releasing the children locked up down the hallway.

Liv gave her a small nod. She was about to dart for her sword when the door at their back opened and the last person Liv wanted to see entered the room.

# CHAPTER EIGHTEEN

"My love," Lucian said as Chloe strode through the door, her long hair bouncing off her wide butt and her hooker heels making a clapping sound on the floor.

Liv's nose twitched from the sudden mix of Chloe's suffocating perfume and the barrel of burned embers sitting before them. They still hadn't figured out what Lucian had been burning. She thought it was probably worth figuring out, but things had just gotten more complicated, with Chloe the Succubus entering the picture. That was the cute little pet name Liv had come up with for Chloe on the fly, and it seemed to fit as the witch wrapped her arms around the bald dictator, kissing him with more passion than was necessary in front of company she didn't know—or even if she did.

The vixen turned, holding onto Lucian tightly. "Darling?"

Lucian smiled down at Chloe. "Yes, my love?"

"You do realize that two lowly magicians are trying to

deceive you with glamour, right?" Chloe said, narrowing her eyes at Liv.

She stiffened, realizing that if Chloe had a superpower, it was that she could see through glamour.

"What?" Lucian asked, throwing Chloe to the side, his eyes narrowed in contempt. "Show yourself, deceivers."

Alicia was apparently out of tricks because she looked at Liv with an expression that said, "It's your turn."

Liv didn't know what else to do since she was swordless and caught off-guard, so she simply looked at Lucian and shrugged. "I don't know what this tramp is barking about. We're from the New York office."

Chloe batted her eyes and snapped her fingers. "No, they aren't. They are from the shop of that old man I used to shack up with and apparently came to stalk me."

Liv suddenly shrank several inches, her clothes not fitting quite as well anymore. She quickly fixed the problem, changing clothes.

Lucian let out a frustrated sigh, as if he was watching a first grader struggling to do math. "Oh, well this is incredibly tiring. You came all the way here to check up on Chloe because of some rivalry over a boy?"

Liv took a step forward, throwing back her cape. "Wrong. I'm a Warrior for the House of Fourteen, and you and your love are under my authority for breaking pretty much every law ever."

The horror that crossed Chloe and Lucian's face was worth keeping the secret until this moment. However, Liv realized her tiny mistake. Her sword was lying on the other side of the metal barrel of smoking embers, which wasn't anywhere close to her grasp.

"Deceitful little jerk," Chloe said through clenched teeth. And for being a chunky little witch, she was surely fast at kicking the barrel of ashes in Alicia and Liv's direction, blanketing them in soot and smoke.

Liv coughed, thinking her lungs were going to come right out of her mouth, then she regained her senses, quickly sucking all the ashes into a container she'd conjured. Alicia still was hacking up her lungs when the air was clear.

Liv swung one way and then the other, looking for Chloe and Lucian.

"They've gotten away," Alicia said, regaining her ability to breathe.

Liv nodded, realizing how quickly things had gone to hell.

Alicia winked. "Good thing I put those locks on the entrances to this building." Liv heard loud snapping sounds emanating from under her feet.

Her eyes shot down before she pulled up her chin to stare are her friend. "Did you…"

"Lock every exit out of this building?" Alicia asked. "Why, yes."

"Can I just say that you are a genius?"

# CHAPTER NINETEEN

L iv grabbed Bellator off the stupid stand-up desk. She didn't know why the gnome didn't just take a walk around the warehouse every few hours. She probably wouldn't have been so harsh on him if he wasn't dating the succubus known as Chloe. Oh, and also didn't abuse old mortals and take advantage of every opportunity he could find.

Liv was very grateful to have her sword back in her hands and not be a meaty man with a breathing problem. She took the lead, bolting out of the office. They were sprinting past the other two doors when Liv halted suddenly, making Alicia slam into her back.

She turned to her friend. "Hey, we have to free the children. Will you be in charge of leading them to safety? I'm afraid that if they stay in here much longer, they will get hurt."

Alicia pulled something out of her bag and nodded. "I'm on it, boss."

"I'm supposed to know what that is, aren't I?" Liv asked, pointing at what Alicia was holding.

The scientist blushed. "Oh, yeah. Sorry. I was going to cut a way out of the facility with this since we can't portal and the exits are blocked. I'll stun whoever is holding the children hostage in there and lead them out of here while you battle Lucian and his hooligans."

Liv nodded, grateful she'd brought a genius along with her. She held her finger above the button to the first door. "I'll stun this hooligan to help you out. How about that?"

Alicia smiled, holding her own hand in front of the locking disk of the door next to Liv's. "Sounds great."

"One, two, three," Liv said and smashed her finger on the small dot. The door unlocked at once, and she kicked it open. She immediately froze, piecing everything they'd heard that day together.

Backing out of the room, she met Alicia in the hallway. The scientist was wearing the same horrified expression as she was.

"Oh!" Liv said, realization strong in her voice. *"Leprechauns!"*

"No no no!" Alicia yelled, horrified. She must have gotten the same education about leprechauns Liv had. They were mean little monsters who stole and thieved, unconcerned for the ones they pillaged. Based on the angry looks on the little red faces, she was guessing her education had been correct. The heathen who had been guarding them didn't look as mean as the little orange-haired guys who had tied him up. On the tables in front of the leprechauns were piles and piles of money that they appeared to be counting.

The little jerks turned their beady, vengeful eyes on the open door. "Get her!" they yelled, and a second later, Liv heard dozens of tiny feet thundering in her direction.

She picked up Alicia and hauled her off the floor, pulling her toward the stairs. There was no way out for anyone but them, which meant they'd better get there first or they'd have to fight their way out. If that happened, it was probably going to be a bloodbath.

## CHAPTER TWENTY

Once Liv got to the bottom of the stairs, she realized it *was* going to be a bloodbath. The hallway that separated them from the exit was filled with angry and hostile magicians.

Liv halted halfway from the bottom. "So, can you cut us out an exit from here?" she asked Alicia.

"Well, I can, but it will just put us into another room. We'll have to keep cutting since we're in the interior of the building."

Liv glanced behind them at the dozens of angry leprechauns holding tiny fists and canes in the air. Their red hair made their heads look to be on fire, which contrasted with their paper-white skin.

"I don't think we can retreat upstairs, where we might have a closer wall to the exterior," Liv stated.

Alicia nodded, gulping with fear. "No, I think we'll have to battle our way out of here."

"Which is fine since you have something spectacular in that bag of tricks to help us," Liv said hopefully.

Pressing her lips together, Alicia shook her head. "I'm sorry, but I'm all about covert tech. I don't design anything that destroys."

Liv nodded, appreciating this about her diplomatic and peaceful friend even at this moment. "Okay, as promised, I will take care of combat. You've done your job."

She took a step forward, and Alicia caught her by the shoulder. "What am I supposed to do?"

Liv glanced at the angry redheads at their backs. "Throw some bright lights and rainbows at them. Redheads can't deal with anything full of sunshine or happiness."

"You got it," Alicia said as Liv bolted in the direction of the angry mob. She was outnumbered and facing a bunch of magicians hyped up on reserves gleaned from helpless mortals. But she had the one thing they didn't: a real purpose.

No one was getting out of there alive unless she allowed it.

She held Bellator at the ready, gritting her teeth as she glared at the meathead leading the pack. "This is for you, Mom!"

# CHAPTER TWENTY-ONE

L iv was grateful to not have meaty arms and a large torso as she barreled forward. She jumped onto the wall to the right, bringing Bellator's hilt down on the head of the first and largest brute. He fell under her feet, making like a magic carpet as she strode down his back and brought her foot up and across the next magician's face.

It was a toothless woman, and she didn't smile when Liv knocked her to the floor. The next several moves were a blur, mostly led by Bellator, who told her where to strike and when. She felt like an avatar in a game, doing what the controller told her to do. But she didn't question the commands, realizing that it was a gift that she felt these instructions from Bellator. Only a Warrior who had connected with their sword was granted that boon in battle.

Bellator was helping her, telling her how to react before the moment arrived. Still, in the back of her mind, she knew it couldn't last. Akio had told her that a good sword did this only to prepare a warrior for the next battle. Liv's job was to preserve her strength while acting like a robotic soldier, responding to all of Bellator's commands.

She faced a magician with a fake eye and half a chin when Bellator's blade dipped toward her feet, no longing leading the battle.

*So you're done, then*, Liv thought, daring to glance down at the sword that seemed to be resting. She brought it back up with a loud roar as the man charged at her.

*Okay, my turn*, Liv thought, turning to the wall, blocking the man on one side and the other one on the other side of him. Like buffoons, they slammed into each other, hitting each other in the noggin.

Liv yanked the sword from the wall, elbowing the next attacker in the face and sending a blast of wind at everyone at their backs. They fell into each other like a pile of dominos. She seized her moment and ran up the side of the narrow hallway, gaining as much speed as she could, and using her magic to increase her height. When she started to descend, the rebels were just rising. Liv came down bouncing between the narrow walls, which seemed to now be positioned for her success. She kicked again and again, jumping back and forth over the heads of the crowd and knocking each one down. When she reached the end of the line, she threw Bellator over her head straight through the crowd. On cue, like the band of villains and she had rehearsed it, they all ducked, some of their shirts getting snagged on the blade roaring overhead.

Alicia turned on cue, summoned by the magic imbued in Bellator, and caught the blade, her eyes wide with disbelief.

Liv kept her excitement at bay and instead stood

straight. "Follow the woman on the stairs unless you want the next pass of the sword to take off your heads."

All the brutes grunted, filing past Alicia and into the room where the leprechauns had been kept and apparently were now. After the last one passed her, Alicia looked at Liv tentatively.

"Are you sure about—"

"Throw me my sword," Liv commanded.

Alicia awkwardly turned the sword around and held it in both her hands. Then she threw it. The blade should have hit the floor with a clatter, and it almost did, but then it peeled upward, sailing toward Liv until she caught it in one hand. She turned with the momentum, a smile on her mouth.

"You got this, Alicia," Liv said, nodding in the direction of the roomful of prisoners.

"And you?" Alicia asked, indicating the rest of the warehouse, where Lucian and his tramp were hiding.

"Don't worry about me," Liv said confidently. "But do call John for backup. We'll need it to take these jerks into custody."

With that, Liv turned toward the last room, where Lucian and Chloe had to be hiding.

She held Bellator at the ready, happier than ever to have this sword at her side.

It was time to end things with the Renegades once and for all.

# CHAPTER TWENTY-TWO

Guinevere Beaufont had taught Liv many things about being a warrior in the short amount of time they'd had together.

Liv knew there were many things her mother had not passed on to her but had meant to. The lessons she had passed on flowed from Bellator's hilt into Liv's body somehow, revitalizing her in a way she'd never felt before, reminding her of her mother's essence.

Liv ran past the many doors in the long hallway, checking each room for the two remaining Renegades.

Lesson number one her mother taught her was, keep your eyes open and your mouth shut.

Liv continued to search, hardly making any noise as she pivoted between each doorway. Was this how her mother had felt on cases? Like she was invincible and close to reaching a conclusion? It was a fine line, but Liv loved every part of it. She felt like it connected her to her mother in a way they'd never had when she was alive. For some reason, at that moment, she knew Guinevere better than she had when her mother was with her.

Her mother loved adventure. She loved feeling alive. But she felt guilty because she loved fighting more than taking care of children. Her mother wanted to bring down the bad guys more than she wanted to tuck her children in at night.

Bellator's hilt pressed into her chest, and Liv felt the realization so strongly it hurt. She wasn't sure how she was getting this insight since this wasn't her mother's sword, but she knew it to be true. As the hilt rested against her breastbone, she knew something very plainly.

That guilt had been with Guinevere every single night that her babies lay in their beds. She'd rather fight crime than be a caregiver. That was Liv's mother's darkest secret, and now she knew it.

Liv threw her back up against a wall, breathing hard. "It's okay, Mommy. I get it."

Guinevere might not have been the best at packing snacks or doing math lessons, but she'd taught Liv other things.

Hearing a commotion down the hall, Liv bolted from her resting place, thinking about another lesson her mother had taught her.

She remembered it as her boots quickly paced across the slick concrete: "Never let them get the upper hand," her mother's voice recited in her ears.

Liv quickly sent a spell at the door fifteen yards ahead. When she knew she was close to the last room, Liv slid into a corner near the doorway, taking time to breathe.

She pulled Bellator up, resting her head against the

blade, the same bit of metal that had killed so many but strangely brought her peace. That was when she heard the last message from her mother.

"Never, ever, my child, let them know how strong you are," Guinevere said in her mind, and suddenly Liv's vision filled with an image of her mother facing the despicable Lucian.

She'd announced she was coming to kick his ass. When she swept down from the top of the warehouse, he'd taken her by surprise, knowing she was there, having heard her. And he knew she had an elven sword, and that she was a Warrior.

Liv awoke from this strange image, realizing what she had to do. Her mother's mistakes wouldn't be hers. Her mother had announced her presence and her gifts, and she'd let them get the upper hand. The story wouldn't be repeated.

Pivoting sharply, Liv did the one thing she knew Lucian wouldn't expect. She released the locks she'd applied to the door to the outside. The one Alicia had reinforced.

Liv stepped into the doorway, watching as Chloe's mouth opened wide with relief when the door was flung open. Lucian threw her into the corner as he raced for freedom. Chloe's expression of hurt might have been enough to disarm some, but Liv simply used her magic to throw ropes around her, binding her limbs as she levitated her into the air. Then she stalked out the door after the man who had battered her mother.

# CHAPTER TWENTY-THREE

L ucian tried many times to create portals as he ran from the building, but thankfully his own magic was working against him. He had kept portal magic off his property, and now he couldn't get away from it.

He looked over his shoulder at her as he ran. His legs seemed to lift off the ground as he sprinted, trying his best to get away. Liv crossed her arms over her chest, knowing exactly how she'd deal with this villain.

When he'd gotten a comfortable distance away, Liv held up her hand and drew him back, as if he'd hit a moving wall that was pushing him toward her. Three times, Liv released him, allowing him to run away before she pulled him back.

Each time she let him go, he grunted with relief, like he was actually going to get away the next time, but all Liv had to do was lift him into the air and pull him back. She did this many more times, watching him get farther away before yanking him in again. It was fun, and she relished it.

Finally, she drew him to within three yards of her and he said, "You've won. What do you want?"

Liv tilted her head toward him, trying to understand this weird specimen. "That's the thing. You seem to think this is a situation where one of us wins and the other loses."

"Well, isn't it?!" Lucian screamed, trying to put his feet on the ground but not finding it since he was suspended in the air.

Liv shook her head. "No, the thing you don't understand is, this isn't a game. This is life. There are some of us who want everyone to live, and others like you who don't care."

"It shouldn't matter!" Lucian yelled.

Liv walked around the man who had tortured her mother. Hurt her. Trapped her like a bird. "That's the thing —it always matters. And for those who refuse to preserve life, there will always be consequences."

"Says who?" Lucian asked like he was talking to his legion of soldiers. "You're wrong. You're nothing compared to me. You need to bow to me." He held out his hand to her, trying to use the same magic trick she had used to keep him from departing. It wasn't going to work on Liv, though, because she had thought to shield herself with a protective spell before running after him, but she didn't want him to know that.

Liv nodded obediently, feeling the essence of her mother in her bones, feeling something ancient awaken inside of her. It directed her like a primal instinct. Her mother's lessons ran through Liv's head, but not in a language she understood.

Instead, her mother's words spilled through her consciousness like the symbols in the House of Fourteen, but she understood them plainly. Liv would keep her eyes open and her mouth shut. She wouldn't let this enemy get the upper hand, and she wasn't going to let this one know how strong she was.

She'd use his ego against him.

"Sure thing, bud. I'll kneel to you," Liv said, and she went to one knee and stuck Bellator into the ground next to her.

She felt the hilt pulse hot in her hands.

"That's right, you will." Lucian laughed, firmly believing he had made her do this.

His evil delight filled the night air, but Liv blocked that out as something strange vibrated in Bellator. She wasn't sure how, but it seemed to be absorbing his spell. And then her mouth opened and words she hadn't meant to say flowed out, "But you, Lucian, will bow to the greatness of the Warrior."

Whatever magic happened next, she didn't know, but she didn't question it because the man in front of Bellator screamed, his laughter ending abruptly. Lucian's hands flew to his face as it contorted.

His screams were loud and full of agony, but Liv didn't take her hand off Bellator to cover her ears. Instead, she held firm to the hilt, hearing a strange chanting echoing from the blade. Liv wasn't sure, but it seemed like it might be the language of the founders.

Maybe she was losing her mind like the man before her, who writhed in pain as he shrank toward the ground. Then, like he was vapor rather than having mass, he was sucked into the blade she held like a genie going into a bottle.

The hilt burned in her hands, and the ground shook under her feet. Holding the sword as it sucked in the man before her seemed impossible, but Liv told herself over and over that she could do it.

Something amazing had happened that night. Something to do with her mother. Something to do with being a Warrior, which was triggered by Bellator, a true Warrior's blade. Liv was certain that for all her life, what had happened on this night would make her a better Warrior.

Blue smoke like the ash in Lucian's office swept through the air and wrapped around the sword as the last of Lucian disappeared into it. Bellator jerked into the air as if trying to escape her grip. Liv didn't let go even though the sword hauled her up to her feet, which barely touched the ground as it rose.

Kicking her legs, Liv tried to pull Bellator back, but the sword was winning the struggle. What had started as a game had shifted to a type of magic she'd never witnessed before. Liv didn't know what to do. She looked over her shoulder, searching for options and saw Alicia bolting in her direction through the darkened grounds. Her friend arrived beside her as her feet rose even higher, like Liv was holding onto a runaway kite. She thought Alicia might leave her after seeing the chaos and the glowing blue blade, but instead, she jumped, grabbing Liv's feet, wrapping her arms around them, and tugging her down several inches.

This brought her back all the way to the ground, but again, Bellator, wrapped in the strange blue smoke that had been Lucian, began to pull them both into the air as if it were bent on taking flight.

"We have to seal the sword," Liv said, not sure where that notion had come from but knowing it was true.

"Okay!" Alicia yelled.

Whatever had opened up in Bellator to swallow Lucian needed to be closed again. That was the only way to contain the horrible man who had been sucked into the blade.

Both magicians began muttering spells. Words flowed off Liv's tongue, spells she didn't know how she knew. Her magic seeped from her body with each spell and the blue light around Bellator dimmed until it glowed no more. The sword dropped from the sky, and Liv fell on her friend as the blade hit the ground with a thud and rolled to the side, normal once more.

With a ragged breath, Liv scooted off Alicia, cautiously glaring at Bellator.

Reading her expression, Alicia asked, "Is it over?"

Carefully, Liv reached for the hilt, expecting it to be hot to the touch like before. It was as cool as the concrete under it. A tingle shot through Liv's fingers, but it didn't disarm her. Instead, it sent a very powerful message that she understood without knowing how.

Bellator had swallowed Lucian, imbuing its blade with a magic that was as old as time. It had everything to do with the lessons her mother had taught her, and Liv realized those teachings hadn't been created by her mother. They were the Creed of the Warrior. Those were the words she'd heard in the founders' language. They'd opened up a space inside Bellator, whose name meant "warrior."

As she held the hilt to her body, she heard a plain and clear message radiate from the sword. "Your enemies are my spirit. I'll use them to fight those you encounter in the future."

This distinctly reminded her of Rory's grandfather's sword Turbinger. It was also a giant-made sword and retained the memory of every battle within it. Liv realized now that it retained more than that.

She proudly regarded the sword in her hands, grateful to learn another of its secrets. She and Bellator had many more battles and enemies to fight together, and she had the founders on her side. She also had her mother's spirit guiding her. Even though none of those forces were alive, they were with her.

# CHAPTER TWENTY-FOUR

C learing out the warehouse had been like cleaning out a graveyard. The Renegades were disgusting and cruel people.

The leprechauns? Well, they weren't scared children like they'd thought. They had been in cahoots with the Renegades and therefore would face similar punishments. The Warriors who had been able to show up to help had confiscated thousands of dollars that the two groups had stolen.

Thanks to Alicia's genius, the hordes of bad guys who had wanted to escape had been stopped. They had simply sat, staring at images too difficult for them to understand or trying to open unopenable locks on toilet seats. The whole thing had been extremely funny when the team called to take them in had shown up.

"Wow," Stefan said, watching a burly man trying to swirl the toilet seat to the right three times for a combination lock. "To think that I could have been doing anything other than this."

SARAH NOFFKE & MICHAEL ANDERLE

"But the Mortal Seven you were after?" Liv asked as he apprehended the bad guy and expertly pulled him up from the ground.

"I did that and still had time to do this, which was much more fun," Stefan told her. "Everything with you is way more fun."

Liv smiled at him, careful to blank her face before another Warrior, Trudy, walked around the corner.

"Looks like everyone is in custody except that Chloe girl," Trudy said. "She states that before she goes into the holding pen, she wants a word with you and the other girl, whoever that is."

Liv smiled, waving over Alicia, who had been hanging out doing perimeter checks or some other nerdy stuff.

"What does she want?" Alicia asked as they neared Chloe, who was trying to bust out of the chains holding her to the side of the warehouse.

"She wants what we all want," Liv stated, staring at Chloe from a few feet away. "Freedom."

Liv shook her head, kicking at the dirt in front of her, feeling Bellator pulsing at her side. "The thing is that some of us deserve to be free, and the rest? Well, they deserve a jail cell so they won't hurt those with the privilege of freedom."

"You know John!" Chloe pleaded, holding onto the chains that bound her. "He wouldn't want me to be imprisoned. He would stop this. Call him. Ask him. He'll tell you I'm a good person."

Liv glanced at Alicia, and a knowing expression passed between them. Liv nodded to her.

Alicia strode forward, careful to keep her distance from

the chained woman. "The thing is, it was your former husband John who put you in this position."

Chloe shrieked, obviously hurt by this statement.

Alicia spun, vengeance making her expression passionate. "That's right. You hurt his people. He's not a mortal you can take advantage of, and neither are any of the others."

"Oh, come on! They are just dumb humans!" Chloe complained.

Alicia turned to Liv, shaking her head. "You ready to take over?"

"I'll try," Liv said, "But sometimes you can rehabilitate them, and sometimes you can't." Liv held up Bellator, looking like she was about to bring the blade down on Chloe

The coward shrank to the ground, covering her head. "No! Just put me away. I'm sorry. I'll do no more wrong."

Liv swung the sword to the side, striding next to her friend and gesturing to Emilio to take the prisoner away. She looked at the sword that was her strength and power. Her connection to everything. Liv smiled at it, uttering a silent prayer.

*Mom, I'll always keep my eyes open and mouth shut. I'll never let them get the upper hand. And I'll never, ever, let them know how strong I am.*

# CHAPTER TWENTY-FIVE

Liv could read the ancient language now without the warrior ring. Before, she had been able to make out a few symbols that she had read before, but something had changed inside her after the battle with Lucian. She felt like a true Warrior now. Something had awoken, and Liv could only dream about what it could mean for her future.

Standing in the hallway of the House of Fourteen, Liv knew exactly what the symbols written in blood on the wall said. The cold draft circling through the darkened corridor wasn't what had her hair standing on end.

"Well?" Plato asked from beside her.

It was rare that she knew something he didn't.

Shivering, Liv wished there was a tiny edge of doubt about what the symbols meant, but there wasn't. "It says we're doomed."

"Is that the paraphrased version?" Plato asked. "Because I'm going to need you to tell me what it says verbatim."

Covering her nose against the smell of rot that filled the

entryway of the House, Liv tried to breathe through her mouth. "It says, 'the God Magician has doomed the world.'"

"'God Magician?'" Plato asked speculatively. He looked at where the Black Void used to be.

"I'm guessing you're not familiar with that person?" Liv questioned.

He shook his head. "We haven't met at any dinner parties. I would have remembered that moniker."

He stared unblinking at where the Black Void had been, and Liv waved her hand in front of his face. "What is it?"

For the first time ever, she saw the lynx shiver. "Something is stirring in the House."

Liv couldn't help but laugh. "The entryway looks like a place on Skid Row, the founders have said the world is doomed, and the swirling blackness has disappeared. I'd say something has more than been stirred up around here."

"You're wrong, though," Plato corrected, still staring at where the Black Void had been. "It hasn't disappeared. I see that now."

"What do you mean?" Liv asked.

"It's spread. The Black Void is covering the House. Whatever was in it isn't just out now. It has taken over."

"Clark said it was a refuge for the founders," Liv stated, the shiver growing more violent, shaking her insides and making her teeth chatter. "Could Adler be back? Decar, maybe?"

"I don't know," Plato answered.

"Maybe it's another founding family," Liv hypothesized.

"God Magician," Plato said mostly to himself.

"This God Magician has doomed the world," Liv repeated the words she'd read. "Like a supreme ruler? Did we mess up? Not assemble the Mortal Seven in time? What could we have done so wrong that we've been sentenced to what sounds like hell?"

The floor under their feet shook.

Liv had rarely seen that look in Plato's eyes. The almost-timeless being was petrified.

She was too. Without knowing how, Liv was aware that whoever the God Magician was, it was there and it was angry.

# CHAPTER TWENTY-SIX

L iv expected the Chamber of the Tree to look much like the entry of the House of Fourteen, so she was surprised to find it bursting with life in a way she'd never seen before.

The bench of council members was absolutely full, with four new faces staring at her in bewilderment. A bird flew over one of the newbies' heads. Sitting on the shoulder of a young man was a small mouse. Liv assumed the other two mortals had their chimeras beside them or sitting in their laps.

They'd assembled the entire Mortal Seven. She didn't understand why they were doomed. That was supposed to protect the House, but it appeared to have made everything worse. Had she misunderstood? Had Adler been right to brainwash mortals into not being able to see magic? Had separating the Mortal Seven from the House been what had preserved it?

She was missing a very important detail.

Taking her place beside Stefan, she noticed something

peculiar. The spot where Decar had stood beside her was illuminated. It had been dim since the evil magician had been killed by Rory and Bermuda. Liv frowned at the circle and looked at Stefan. "Have we replaced the Sinclairs?"

He shook his head. "I don't think so, but I've been busy taking care of the New York office of the Renegades."

"Thank you," Liv said as Clark stood, making the chamber go silent.

"As you can see, the Mortal Seven have all been recovered," Clark began, a unique authority in his voice that Liv had never heard him use before. "Liv was also successful at shutting down the Renegades, although she went off without orders from the council."

"Did I?" Liv asked innocently, looking at John guiltily.

"The New York Renegades have been shut down," Clark continued. "But this situation has brought up something important that has bothered many of us for quite some time."

Lorenzo slammed his hand on the bench, his face red. "Magicians need to have their magic registered."

"I disagree," Clark countered. "This group assembled because they didn't want to be controlled by us."

"That's not true," Liv cut in, making both men whip around to face her. She knew she wasn't going to make Clark very happy with her next statements, but she'd thought long and hard about them. "The Renegades assembled because they don't want to follow our laws. They wanted to exploit and hurt others for their own gains."

"But we've struggled for a long time to get magicians to register their magic," Clark stated, leaning forward.

"Yes, and that's because they're the only magical race required to do so," Liv stated.

"You're not going to make the argument again that other races should join the House?" Lorenzo asked, irritation in his voice.

"I'm not only proposing that, but also many other changes to our House structure," Liv offered. "The laws that make up this organization are outdated at best. They are archaic. As Royals, we're not allowed to mix our genes with other races, which only perpetuates the prejudice they feel toward us." She saw a satisfied grin flash onto Emilio's face.

"Oh, this is hardly the time to discuss this," Bianca interrupted. "Father Time is missing. Don't you have more important things to do?"

Liv opened her mouth to respond, but something deep within her made her keep her words locked away. It was like she was operating from a new place of knowing all of a sudden, ever since the battle with Lucian.

"We should always have time to fix laws that don't serve us or the magical world," Stefan stated, picking up Liv's argument. "Those laws prevent the races from mixing. They prevent Royal families from intermarrying if they so choose. They keep us locked in small boxes, and then we wonder why no one wants to follow our rules? The rest of the world doesn't see us as a just organization. Maybe they are more respectful of us now since we've incorporated the Mortal Seven, but they still see us as overly conservative, enforcing outdated laws instead of upholding justice."

"Why does this council's attention need to be monopolized by dating issues, Mr. Ludwig?" Bianca asked, her tone severe.

"Because it reflects on our reputation," Stefan answered at once.

"He's right," Emilio joined in. "The other races don't respect us—"

"That's quite enough, brother," Bianca interrupted. "I'm fully aware of your viewpoint on this matter."

"But the rest of us are not," Hester stated. "Why is this coming up now? What do we the council not know?"

As terrified as Liv had been to step into the Chamber of the Tree a moment ago, she was pleasantly surprised by how this was going. They were making progress. Laws were being discussed, which was the first part of changing things. Maybe the founders were wrong. Maybe they weren't doomed. Maybe it just felt like that because the things that they had established all those centuries ago were shifting and that was scary. The foundation of the House was being rocked, and for those who had created it, that would be upsetting. But for the current generation, it was a much-needed change.

Jude and Diabolos appeared on either side of the bench, both with their heads down and a strange intensity in their eyes. Liv couldn't pull her gaze from them for several long moments until Emilio stole her attention.

He stepped forward, staring straight at his sister. "Not only do I agree with Warrior Beaufont that the laws need to be changed, but I also know why we need to incorporate other races votes into our dealings."

Bianca had never before looked so angry, her pinched

face making her look like a withered turnip. "Em, I urge you to stop this nonsense."

"I used to be like you, sister," Emilio continued. "I thought we were better than the other races. I didn't think we needed them to maintain our rule. But this world is changing, and we can't do it alone anymore. The other races want what we have always had to offer—protection for magic. But they want to be included. I have it on good authority from the fae that they won't stand for being ignored any longer. They don't need to be on the council, but they want to be included somehow."

A startled scream shot out of Bianca's mouth. Liv's first thought was that it was in protest to her brother finally standing up to her.

Then she noticed that the tree behind them was fully illuminated with the names of all of the Mortal Seven. That was not what sucked all the breath out of her lungs. It wasn't even that Jude and Diabolos fell beside the bench, both appearing to have fainted. Liv hoped that was all and that they weren't dead.

What had stolen Liv's breath was that on the tree, shining brighter than all the other names, was "Sinclair."

# CHAPTER TWENTY-SEVEN

L iv realized that every single member of the council was staring at something behind her. She tensed, feeling Stefan beside her do the same.

In unison, every one of the Warriors drew their weapons, spinning to face what stood at their backs. Liv had Bellator in her hands but hadn't turned fully when her face careened into the ground. Stefan's shoulder rammed into her face as he toppled onto her. The sound of Akio, Emilio, and Trudy falling over, their weapons clattering to the stone floor, gave her little reassurance that they'd been successful where she and Stefan had failed.

All Liv knew for sure was that she was paralyzed. She could blink and breathe, but that was all. That was why, as she looked into Stefan's face, next to hers, she didn't say a word. His expression communicated his own fear effortlessly.

Like Jude and Diabolos, something had taken out all six Warriors in the chamber. Whatever could do that wasn't something she wanted to face.

As if privy to her thoughts, a voice said, "Rise."

It wasn't someone she recognized unless the devil had a voice. Not that she'd ever heard it speak before, but that was what it reminded her of.

"Rise!" the voice commanded again, and Liv jumped up, realizing she could move.

She pushed to her feet and faced a figure straight out of her nightmares. Standing in the center of the chamber was a man in long white robes, the hems surrounded by crawling and wiggling lizards and snakes. They climbed over the hem of the robe and under it, making it billow as if being blown by the wind. The man had hair that hung down to the floor behind. It was the same color as his robes, and his eyes were indiscernible since they appeared to be two beams of light that shone on everything he looked at. Currently, he was running his gaze over each of the Warriors in turn, momentarily blinding them.

Liv didn't know how, but she was absolutely certain this was the God Magician. Her eyes swept to Jude and Diabolos, who were stirring like the Warriors. On the bench, the Councilors were all looking down at the man in the center of the chamber with extreme trepidation. Clark's eyes connected with Liv's and he shook his head slightly, fear covering his face.

"I am Talon Sinclair, a founder of the House of Seven," the man began, his tone making Liv cringe in a way she had never done before. She'd faced the hellhound and soulless men and leagues of zombies and demons, and yet this small, frail man filled her with a terror she'd never known before. "For centuries, I've laid dormant, instructing my relatives how best to run the place I made into what it was. However, you have ruined it all!"

His voice shook the floor under their feet, throwing Liv into Stefan. He caught her but nearly tumbled face-first in the process.

"No more!" Talon yelled, snapping his fingers. Each of the Mortal Seven fell forward, their heads hitting the table in front of them.

Liv bolted forward but Talon held out a hand, stopping her. The smell that radiated from the not-quite-man made her stomach curdle.

"Warriors for the House of Seven, I've shown you that simply by my will, I can paralyze you," the man before them said. "You have been warned. Any attempts on my life will result in your death. I've not killed these revolting mortals you've brought into this chamber. Their chimeras prevent me from doing so. But they will sleep for as long as it takes us to right what you've caused to go wrong."

With every part of her being, Liv wanted to kill the man before her, but she knew she couldn't. Something very important was stopping his defeat. It was why he'd come out of the Black Void and had the power to take over the House.

Her mouth popped open. Papa Creola! Of course. He prevented beings from living past their time, but if he was gone... If someone had done something to him, Talon could rise. He could take over the House once more.

Liv stepped back to her spot, earning a nod of approval from Talon.

"So," he said, turning to face the council, his eye beams running over each of them. "I am the God Magician. I made this House what it was, and it will return to that. I will see to it. There will be no changes to the laws. There will be no other races allowed in this place. There will only be my rule, and it will be absolute!"

Dust rained from the ceiling as Talon's voice boomed, making Liv's chest vibrate. She'd always stood up for what she believed and challenged that which was wrong, but at that moment, she was ready to do whatever the man before her said. That was how afraid she was of the God Magician.

To Liv's surprise, it was Clark who stood, staring down at Talon. "How are you still alive?"

The God Magician faced her brother. "Simple. I killed your ancestor." He then looked at Haro. "And yours. And the others who have since been replaced. I'm the strongest magician ever to live. I saw a future for the House that the others didn't want to accept. Mortals didn't belong here with us, ruling. They belong as our slaves or abolished from the planet, but they should have no say in the world of magic."

Liv usually would have argued, spouting off in her sarcastic manner, but she knew better. Talon was no ordinary magician. He was too powerful. He couldn't be stopped. And that meant the founders were right: The God Magician would doom this world.

# CHAPTER TWENTY-EIGHT

"What do you mean, he's asleep?" Alicia nearly yelled when Liv told her the news about John and the other Mortal Seven.

"He's fine," Liv answered. "Pickles is with him and is keeping him alive, as are all the other chimeras with their mortals."

"But for how long?" Alicia asked.

Liv looked at Stefan and Clark. Reading the expressions on their faces, she simply shrugged. "We don't know. This is new territory."

"Alicia, we couldn't move him," Clark explained. "Talon wouldn't allow it. He told us the mortals were to remain where they were."

"So what are you doing about this?" Alicia paced in Liv's apartment, nearly tripping over her feet from stress.

"Talon sent the Warriors on missions," Liv began. "The council has been tasked with figuring out how to do other things."

"Missions?" Alicia questioned, her voice rising. "Other things?"

Liv cringed, squinting as she peered at Stefan. "He's ordered the Warriors to kill the rest of the Mortal Seven families. The council is supposed to be researching how to get rid of the current Mortal Seven."

Alicia yelled in frustration.

"We're not doing it, though," Stefan explained. "We're only pretending to. Well, we're not doing it until he kills one of us."

Liv shot him a look that said, "That didn't help."

"Apparently, when he got rid of the Mortal Seven the first time, it was easier because he'd murdered the founders," Clark explained.

"So why doesn't he just do that?" Alicia asked, earning offended looks from the three.

"Well, thanks," Liv answered. "We think he isn't strong enough to take us all out. He needs us to help him. But although he can't murder us, he *can* incapacitate us. That gives us hope that Papa Creola is still alive somewhere. If he is, we can fight Talon, but we have to find Papa Creola first."

"I don't understand." Alicia sat on Liv's couch, placing her head in her hands.

"We don't either," Stefan related. "Most of this is conjecture, and we're pretty sure that if we do everything that Talon asks, he'll grow more powerful and kill us anyway."

"Then why do it?" Alicia yelled.

Liv shot her brother a sideways look. "Well, we're not. Not entirely, anyway. The council is looking into what

Talon asked, as well as trying to figure out how to rebuild a new signal that will stop mortals from seeing magic again."

"So things are going back to the way they were before?" Alicia was irate now, shaking and crying.

"No, we just appear to be doing what he says," Clark said consolingly. "We're not really doing it, or if we are, we're doing it extremely slowly."

"Then what are you doing to stop this?" Alicia asked.

Right on cue, the doorbell rang.

Liv didn't turn. Instead, she simply snapped her fingers. A moment later, she heard several pairs of feet enter her apartment. All she needed was the surprised look on Alicia's face to know that the people she'd expected had come in to stand behind her.

Liv turned, looking at many people she'd never expected to see in her home. Standing at her back were Bianca and Emilio Mantovani, Lorenzo and Maria Rosario, the Takahashi brothers, the DeVries sisters, and Raina Ludwig. Turning back to Alicia, Liv allowed the first smile to unfurl on her face since she'd learned of this tragedy.

"We're banding together," Liv answered Alicia. She shot a glance at Stefan. "We're coming together in a way we've never had to do before. We're not just the House of Fourteen anymore." Liv looked at the Councilors and Warriors standing in her living room. "We are magicians who will do anything to protect the magical world, even if that means we destroy the very organization we work for."

# CHAPTER TWENTY-NINE

I t was bizarre to see her living room crowded with so many faces, but not any odder than anything else that had happened in the last twenty-four hours.

Thankfully, Clark had advised them of a way to communicate among the members of the House so that Talon was unaware. The council members couldn't be gone long or he'd be suspicious, but something was clear: anything that happened in the House, the God Magician would find out about.

After a lot of collective muttering, the six Warriors and Councilors had determined that Talon had been the one to appoint Adler to his role and make him as powerful as he had been. They'd assumed that on the many occasions Adler or Decar had lied, Talon's power had masked this from the regulators, Jude and Diabolos. They also reasoned that Talon had had something to do with erasing Kayla's name from the tree in the chamber when she hadn't been killed. He most likely had been the one to recruit her. But something was startlingly obvious.

Talon was the only Sinclair left. That was why he'd come out of the Black Void and allowed it to take over the House.

Before everyone had arrived and Alicia had lost it, Stefan had confided in Liv that he'd been duped too. He'd believed that Talon had blocked him from sensing him, since he was usually aware when pure evil was close by, like demons. However, Stefan had never known Talon was in the House. He hadn't seen the Black Void. He'd been as blind as the rest of them, and it pained him now.

Not caring about laws and stupid things that didn't matter anymore, Liv intertwined her hand in Stefan's as Clark began the informal meeting that couldn't last long. "Our first order of business has to be how to get Papa Creola back."

Many of the Councilors and Warriors exchanged confused expressions.

"That's Father Time," Stefan explained.

"Yes, we have to find him. It's more urgent now than it was before," Akio affirmed, looking at Liv.

She shook her head. "I still don't have a lead. I'm hoping to hear something soon, though. The person helping me has everyone working for them searching."

The scared faces of the House members stared at each other. They'd fought before. Bickered. Interrogated each other. But what was threatening them now was more important than being right or beating each other. They all knew without a shadow of a doubt that Talon had to be stopped. No one argued that point. Now it made sense that they'd all passed the lie detector tests. They weren't the ones who had deceived the House, bringing numerous enemies to the surface. It was so clear now. It had always been Talon. He had come after and killed the Beaufonts, Liv's parents and siblings. He had been the mastermind behind everything.

"What are we supposed to do while we wait?" Haro asked.

"The council needs to appear to be cooperative," Liv ordered. "You can't really make progress, but you need to appear that you are."

"And what about the Warriors?" Bianca asked, and for the first time, she didn't sound like a whiny little jerk.

Liv gulped, thinking. "We need to recruit help for when I do locate Papa Creola. I have a feeling this isn't going to be a mission I can complete on my own. I might...no, I'll definitely need your help, as well as others."

"Like who?" Hester asked.

"Well," Stefan stated, "it would be good if we had someone from each of the races. A giant to control the earth element—"

Liv nodded, knowing he was exactly right. "Yes, and we'll need an elf for water."

"Leave that to me," Akio stated. "I've worked with quite a few I trust."

"Okay," Liv agreed. "And I can ask King Rudolf to assign me a fae to help out."

"And what about gnomes?" Trudy asked.

Liv shook her head. "I've got fire magic, thanks to Papa Creola, so we should be okay there." It was hard for her to get out the words, knowing that somewhere in the world, the Father of Time was incapacitated and in need of rescue. Just as he had recently feared, someone had been after him, and they'd succeed in rising as soon as capturing him. But the war wasn't over, and Liv planned on winning it and ending the God Magician for good.

# CHAPTER THIRTY

It was hard for Liv to walk through the crowded casino in Las Vegas, knowing that out in the world, horrible things were happening. She wanted to yell at the drunks pulling on slot machines that Father Time was missing! She felt the need to throw the chips on the high roller tables into the gamblers' faces, telling them that they were in danger simply by being mortal. And then there were those filling their faces with food, who she wanted to smack, but mostly just because they were gorging on food that she really wanted to eat but didn't have the time for.

She chomped off a bite of one of the protein bars Rudolf had sent her to try, chewing it without tasting. Right then, she didn't care for the milk chocolate or flaky coconut or crispy oats. She just needed the sustenance to keep up her magical reserves.

Tasting something that wasn't right, Liv stopped, picking something from her teeth. "Oh, gross. Are those dried peas?" She shook her head, making a mental note to talk to Rudolf about his ingredient choices after all the mortal threats were over, which, if she didn't act fast, might be never.

Liv sped all the way to the top of the Cosmopolitan Casino on the Las Vegas Strip, not slowing until she got to the king's chamber. As they had become accustomed to doing, the guards allowed her entry immediately.

She hustled through the doors, ready to fill Rudolf in about the horror that had befallen the world, but she was stopped by a wad of confetti that exploded in her face upon entering the chambers.

Rudolf threw up his hands, his mouth wide, a paper party hat on his head. "Yay!"

Liv blew out a breath, realizing that pieces of paper were covering her head and face. She tried to regain her composure.

"Wow, that was fast!" Rudolf exclaimed. "I just sent you the announcement like two minutes ago."

Liv realized that her chest was rising and falling rapidly. She brushed off her face and shook her head. "What are you talking about?"

"The invite," Serena answered, stepping up beside Rudolf, wrapping her arms around his waist, and pulling him in tightly. She was also wearing a dumb party hat.

"Again, I realize you all think that answers my question, but it doesn't," Liv stated, feeling her temper rising.

"The. Invitation. To. Celebrate," Rudolf said, articulating each word.

Liv lowered her chin. "Celebrate what?"

The two looked at each other and laughed. Then they halted. Looked at Liv and laughed again. "The announcement of our pregnancy."

Not expecting this, Liv's mouth fell open. She tried to shake her head, to dispel their happiness and tell them why she was there, but she couldn't bring herself to do it. Instead, despite the heartbreak in her chest, she bounded forward, wrapping her arms around both of their necks and pulling them in. "This is great news! Congratulations! I'm so happy for you."

"We're excited too," Serena said when Liv released her. "It came as quite a shock since we'd tried every single fertility trick and it didn't work. But Ru told me you said we should stop worrying so much, so that was what we did. We stopped the treatments, and bam, we were pregnant like the next day."

"That doesn't sound like something I helped with, based on the timing," Liv said doubtfully.

"Yeah, I agree. You definitely could have told us sooner," Rudolf said, tilting his head to the side. "But that's not why you're here."

"Of course it is," Liv said, backing toward the entrance. She'd just have to do this without the fae's help, which shouldn't be a problem since they usually only complicated things with their insistence on bringing so much luggage for wardrobe changes on missions.

"No, it's not," Rudolf retorted. "If it was, you'd have the party hat we included in the invite."

Liv's eyes slid upward. "Oh, well, you know how I hate hats."

"And brushing her hair," Serena said to her husband.

"Stop talking to Bermuda," Liv scolded. "Anyway, I'm very happy for you two. I'll drop the handcuffs off for the baby in a few months. And just remember that eating too

159

many carrots will turn the baby orange, and that as much as you love standing on your head, Serena, it will result in a flat noggin."

Liv turned, intending to race out of the chamber. To her surprise, Rudolf caught her by the wrist with surprising agility. He whipped Liv around, a serious expression on his face.

"That's not why you came," he insisted. "Tell me, Olivia."

Liv snapped her hand from his and shook her head. "Call me that again, and I will send goblins to take your manhood so you can never breed again."

Rudolf backed away quickly, giving Serena a scared look. "I think she has that power. We better not mess with her."

Liv brushed off the rest of the confetti, shaking her head. "Anyway, I'm happy for you both. Congrats. But I've got to be off."

Rudolf reached for her again but stopped as his hand brushed hers. He snapped back to attention when she spun to face him with an angry glare.

"What?" Liv growled.

"I know there's another reason you came here," he explained, looking slightly scared of her.

Liv considered him and then Serena. She didn't want to spoil their news, but what good would it do if Talon rose to full power and destroyed the world? Liv sighed. "Okay, fine. There's an evil power named Talon who was the one behind stopping mortals from seeing magic who has taken the House of Fourteen back over, which he's calling the House of Seven again. He's taken Papa Creola, and we don't know where he is, but when we do, we need to go after him with a team. I was hoping you could give me your best fae to accompany and help us."

Liv drew in a deep breath, awaiting Rudolf's answer.

He seemed stunned by this information, and for a full ten seconds, simply shook his head. "How dare he call it the House of Seven after all the retraining you tried to do?"

Liv rolled her eyes. "He's the one who… You know what, never mind. You get the nursery ready. We will find Papa Creola. Just keep the peas out of the granola bars."

For a second time, Liv tried to turn to leave, but this time, Rudolf appeared on the other side of her, having teleported. Which was incredibly impressive, since making a peanut butter and jelly sandwich was difficult for the fae on a good day. She halted before running into him.

"Oh, no, you don't, Liv Beaufont," he said, wagging a finger in front of her face.

She swiped it out of the way. "Be grateful you have a child on the way. Otherwise, I'd kill you, King Rudolf."

He simply smiled at her. "I want to help. This Talon sounds like a real booger, and I'm not going to stand by while he hurts mortals or the House of Fourteen. Sign the fae up for thirty boxes."

Liv drew in a breath. "You realize this isn't a donation service where you buy a bunch of boxes of cookies from Girl Scouts, right?"

"It's an expression," Serena said, stepping around Rudolf and smiling. "And my husband is right. We are going to help, even if it kills him."

Rudolf nodded at his wife. "And that means I'm the fae who will go into battle with you."

To Liv's shock, Serena continued to nod, like this was a good idea.

She backed away. "Oh, no. You two are going to have a child who will inherit this kingdom. There's no way I'm going to allow you, the soon-to-be-father to the first mortal-slash-fae child, to risk your life in what will probably be the most dangerous mission I've ever been on as a Warrior for the House of Fourteen."

Rudolf sped after her. "No, Liv, you have to understand that I have to do this."

She pulled her hands back, shaking her head. "Then go bungee jumping or ziplining on Freemont. Find another way to get your thrills before the baby comes. This isn't the way."

Rudolf was undeterred and gave her the most serious expression she'd ever seen him wear. "Liv, understand me. I'm not doing this for one last thrill. I want to do this because it's important. What's the point in bringing a child into this world if it's destroyed? And what's the point in being the king of the fae if I'm not going to step up when the time comes to defend my people? This Talon jerk sounds like he needs an ass-kicking, and I want to be the one to give it to him…" He glanced at Serena, a question in his eyes. "If that's okay with you, sweetie?"

Serena smiled and nodded repeatedly. "Yes, Ru."

He returned his gaze to Liv. "Then, there you go. I want to go on your mission to end this big baddie. Please, Liv."

Liv considered his request. She had expected Rudolf to assign her one of his best fae soldiers, not himself, but she had to respect what he said. However, he was her friend and expecting a child and the king of the fae, and she didn't want anything to happen to him. In all honesty, she didn't want anything to happen to anyone she loved, and she was taking many of them on the mission—Stefan, Rory, Akio, Trudy, and many others.

No, Liv decided. She couldn't chance any more friend's lives.

She let out a long breath, trying to figure out how to tell Rudolf. "Look, Rudolf, although—"

"No, *you* look, Warrior Beaufont," Rudolf said, stepping up and pressing his nose against hers. "I'm the king of the fae, and I demand to go on this mission. If you decline, we will pull all support from the House from now until forever. You either allow me to stand beside you as a friend, or you consider me your enemy."

Liv stared eyeball to eyeball at the fae in front of her, trying to figure out how serious he was. When he burst out laughing, spitting on her face from the outburst, she realized she shouldn't discount his seriousness, only his maturity. That was why, when he stood tall again and gave her a stern expression, Liv extended a hand to him.

"If you want to join us, we'd be proud to have you, King Rudolf," she said to her friend.

He looked like he couldn't believe it for a minute, glancing back at Serena several times. Finally, he took her hand and shook it. "I'm happy to fight this battle for the future beside you."

Liv glanced at Serena and winked. "For the future generation, who will one day lead us toward greater things."

# CHAPTER THIRTY-ONE

Bermuda Laurens paced in front of the long dining room table where the Warriors, Alicia, Rory, and Rudolf were seated. There had been a lot of pacing lately, and it did little to help Liv's nerves.

Only a minute prior, Liv had been given the location where Papa Creola was being held and she showed it to Bermuda, believing she'd know the most about the monster who held him hostage.

"Is it Disney World? Is that where Papa Creola is?" Rudolf asked, looking between Liv and Bermuda.

"No. For the tenth time, it's not," Liv sputtered.

The fae shrugged. "It was a good guess, though. I got lost in there for about a quarter of a century, so I could see the same thing happening to Papa Creola."

"He's not lost," Trudy stated, sitting stoically next to Akio.

"No, he's not, but he will be, the longer he stays there," Bermuda said, turning to face the group. She glanced at Liv confidently. "You can get him back, though. I'm convinced of it."

Liv nodded, appreciating the support from the giantess more than ever. She stood and looked down the table. "Papa Creola has been taken by none other than the gorgon Medusa."

"Oh, that witch just doesn't give up, does she? She won't quit until she gets a man," Rudolf said, shaking his head.

"You've met Medusa?" Rory asked beside him.

"Met her? We used to date," Rudolf stated. "That vixen tried a time or two to lure me in with her sexy ways, but I refused to fall for her little tricks."

Liv squinted at the fae. "Medusa? Are you sure?"

He blinked at her. "Oh wait, you said 'the gorgon Medusa'?" Rudolf shook his head. "No, I was thinking of someone else. A siren who also has a head of snakes, Medura. She can't turn someone to stone, but she'll try to make a single part of a man rock-hard, if you know what I mean." He elbowed Rory in the side, but the giant wasn't entertained.

Liv sighed and glanced at Bermuda. "Does he have to go? We don't need a fae, right?"

"You will, actually," she answered. "Ice magic will come in very handy. It can act as a mirror, which is the only way you can look at Medusa without turning to stone."

Alicia tapped her fingers on the table, as restless as the rest of them. "I can create tablets that work like mirrors too. I was also thinking of communication systems for all of you who are going on the mission."

"Although that's a good idea," Bermuda said, actually being complimentary, "it won't work. Medusa has been confined to an island off the coast of Turkey. It's in ancient Aeolis, which was thought by many to be lost. In actuality, it is simply hidden. You'll need the elves' navigation magic to find it. Otherwise, you'll be searching for much longer than Papa Creola has. The longer he's stone, the harder it will be to reverse."

Everyone looked down the table at Akio, who had been in charge of recruiting an elf to go along on the mission. "Unfortunately, none of the elves I spoke with were interested in going along."

"Yes, it's a full moon tonight, and that's not a time when elves want to be away from home. Their powers are diminished severely on those days," Bermuda stated matter-of-factly.

"Wish I would have known that when I was hunting down all those criminal elves to prove our loyalty to the clan," Stefan remarked.

Bermuda threw her hands up. "Did no one read my book?"

"You have a book?" Rudolf asked. "Are there pictures?"

Liv held up her hand, redirecting her attention to Akio. "I can get us to the island since Dakota Sky, the king of the elves, gave me a navigation stone."

The warrior nodded. "And when I asked for their help, they granted me water magic."

"Oh, nice!" Rudolf cheered. "I want to be paired up with a water man if we're going to an island."

Liv shook her head. "No, I think we need to be in teams of two and balance out our skills. Rudolf, you'll be with Rory, because that way you'll have one reflective surface." She indicated Trudy and Akio. "You two will be together, using Akio's water skills as a mirror." Liv glanced at Stefan. "You're with me."

He nodded at once.

"What about us?" Maria Rosario asked, indicating her and Emilio.

She was always so quiet and unassuming that it was easy to forget she was there. Liv hadn't many opportunities to get to know the warrior, not like the others.

"Maria and Emilio, we need to have you Warriors out there doing what Talon ordered, or at least appearing to do so," Liv stated.

"So you want us to go and hunt down the rest of the Mortal Seven families?" she asked.

Liv nodded. "Track them down. Keep an eye on them. Don't let anything happen to them."

"So I shouldn't kill them?" Maria questioned.

Liv tilted her head at the other warrior, squinting like she had misheard her. She finally understood why she hadn't spent much time with Maria; she was nuts. "No, you're not to kill anyone."

"But that's what Talon wants us to do," Maria argued.

"Right," Liv said, drawing the word out. "I want you to *appear* to be doing what he asked, but in actuality, you're going to not kill anyone. Does that make sense?"

Maria shrugged. "Okay, but killing them would be more convincing."

Liv and Stefan exchanged petrified glances. She made a mental note that if they made it out of this alive and the House continued, Maria was going to have a psych evaluation and possibly be replaced.

"All right, you have your orders," Liv said, looking at the

rest of the people at the table. "The rest of you, minus Bermuda and Alicia, I want with me."

Emilio nodded, disappearing from the room.

Maria stood, appearing a bit deflated. "Fine. I'll go track down the Mortal Seven families and not murder them." She left without another word.

Stefan gave the others a speculative look. "Did any of you know that she's crazy?"

Akio shrugged. "I have personally never heard her speak much."

"I thought she was just shy," Trudy added.

"I thought she was rather charming," Rudolf stated. "A real problem-solver."

Liv drew a deep breath, trying to regain her focus. "Okay, we'll all go together, and split up in teams once we're there. I want this to go as quickly as possible. Like Bermuda said, time is of the essence."

"Time." Rudolf laughed. "And we're going to rescue Father Time. Get it?"

Rory shook his head at the fae before turning to Liv. "What about you and Stefan? You don't have a reflective surface."

"She does now," Bermuda said, snapping her fingers.

In front of Liv appeared a beautifully crafted shield that was made up of mirrors set at different angles. Her mouth fell open, which she saw plainly in the reflective surface. "Wow, this is gorgeous," she said, running her fingers over the incredible craftsmanship.

"A bit conceited, isn't she?" Rudolf said to Rory, elbowing him again.

"I believe she's talking about the shield," the giant said, looking at his mum. "Is that Athena's shield?"

Bermuda nodded proudly. "Yes. It was used to defeat Medusa once, and I think it's fitting that it be used a second time. It's been in my personal collection, but I want you, Liv, to have it."

"Thank you," Liv said, still staring at the shield in awe.

"Defeat her once?" Trudy asked. "How is Medusa back?"

"She isn't back," Bermuda stated. "She is confined to the temple where she was sent after her first defeat. It appears that Talon had her awakened. He must have lured Papa Creola there. According to the information given to Liv, Father Time has been turned to stone."

"How can we bring him back from that?" Akio asked.

The giantess gazed at Liv. "I'm not sure, but if anyone can, it will be you people."

# CHAPTER THIRTY-TWO

Pointing at an open patch of crystal-blue water, Liv said, "It's right there."

Akio squinted. "I don't see anything."

"That's the location of Medusa's temple," Liv stated, rereading the navigation stone. "It has to be."

"Could it have sunk?" Stefan asked.

"No, we just can't see it until we set course for it," Rory stated, taking the stone from Liv and handing it to Rudolf, who was at the wheel of his ship, the *Serena*. "Take us there."

"You got it, Skipper," Rudolf chirped. He had been all smiles since getting back on the open water. The ocean suited him.

Liv was grateful that everyone's attention was on the captain and the invisible island. She used that opportunity to pull the note Clark had given her before she'd left from her pocket. There hadn't been time for proper goodbyes or well wishes. As Liv had quickly hugged him and Sophia, he'd slipped the note into her cape pocket.

SARAH NOFFKE & MICHAEL ANDERLE

The paper was damp from the sea air when she unfolded it. The note was brief and to the point, just like her brother Clark.

*Liv,*

*Be careful. Come home safely. We need you, and not just because you're the best Warrior the House has. Without you, I'd be lost.*

Familia est sempiternum

*Clark*

Blinking away the tears in her eyes, Liv held her chin up as salty air blasted her in the face.

"Are you ready for this?" Stefan asked, having appeared beside her soundlessly.

"I don't think it matters much if I'm not," she answered, folding the note from her brother and sticking it back in her pocket. There she found the small package from Papa Creola, the one she was only to open if all hope was lost.

"What is that?" Stefan asked.

"I'm not sure."

He nodded like that made sense. "I often carry around packages I know nothing about too."

"You would," she replied, winking at him. "Papa Creola gave it to me. It's only to be used if I run out of options. Apparently, it's part of his power."

Stefan whistled, shaking his head. "Damn it. That man had to show me up. Looks like I'll have to rethink my birthday gift for you."

Liv laughed. "It also could burn out my magic if I use it."

"And therein lies the reason it's only to be used as a last resort," Stefan stated.

The ship lurched, coming to a swift halt and throwing Liv forward. She caught herself, looking back at Rudolf.

"Ahoy! I've found land!" he exclaimed.

"We see that," Rory called, batting his eyes in annoyance and glaring at Liv. She was pretty certain he was peeved that she'd teamed him up with Rudolf, but it made the most sense. Rudolf's flippant nature would play well with Rory's seriousness. She was learning that teams were best if balanced like that.

Stefan slung his bow over his shoulder, glaring out at the beautiful lush island that had literally appeared out of nowhere. "Unassuming, isn't it?"

The island was small, about the size of a football field. In the center was a large, round building surrounded by columns. "I've learned that 'unassuming' is usually a bad thing," Liv remarked. "I'd be less worried if it was sprawling and had a giant skyscraper."

"Yes, the most dangerous people I know are pretty unassuming," Akio said, taking the place next to Stefan.

"I've heard rumors that the most unassuming dragon rider will soon join the Elite," Trudy stated.

Liv swallowed. She knew the seer hadn't heard any rumors. Trudy had seen it in a vision, and therefore it must be true. Liv couldn't think about that now. Her focus had to be solely on rescuing Papa Creola.

Rudolf rubbed his hands together, then charged past the warriors, jumping over the bow of the ship and landing on the sand. "Come on. What are you waiting for?"

Liv held up her hand. "Follow the king. He's obviously the least reluctant of us."

"Oh, hell," Rudolf whined. "I think I stepped in bird poop."

Stefan winked at her. "You're the real leader here. Good thinking, letting him go first."

# CHAPTER THIRTY-THREE

The Warriors worked like a machine, each remaining vigilant, watching for potential dangers as they made their way across the island to the large white building.

They hadn't worked on a single mission together, but never before had there been a reason for them to join forces. No matter what, Talon Sinclair had to be stopped, and it made sense that Papa Creola was the only one who could do it. Talon had been trying to take him down for weeks, Liv realized now, looking back. Papa was the only one who could keep Talon from rising to power, and once he was back, that power-hungry murderer was going to be stopped. But Liv had to save Papa Creola first.

Cautiously, the group approached the front of the building, Liv taking the lead. She'd been surprised not to encounter a fire breathing dragon or man-eating skeletons rising from the sand. That did little to assure the road ahead would be easy.

Once the group was assembled at the entrance, Liv used her shield to determine if Medusa was in the temple. Her investigation proved the first room of the temple consisted of one room with three doors. Liv swung around the corner, Stefan copying her movements on the other side of the entry.

The temple was beautiful, with an open ceiling and intricately decorated marble floors and walls. In the middle of the round room was a beautiful statue that glowed from the sunlight kissing the top of it.

Liv tensed, realizing what she was seeing in the middle of the temple. "That's not a statue."

Following her line of vision, Stefan kept his bow at the ready while continuing to scan the space.

Liv rushed forward toward the solid form of Papa Creola.

"No!" Stefan yelled. "It could be a trap."

Liv shook her head. "It's not." She wasn't sure how she knew that, but her instincts seemed to be leading her.

Tentatively, she touched the face of the statue. Papa Creola appeared exactly like she remembered with his round cheeks and wide eyes, but he was stone, his mouth open in horror.

Suddenly Liv's chest ached. Not just because she cared about the authoritative little man who always ordered her around and dug into her business, but also because of who he was.

He was the past, the present, and the future. In a blink of an eye, he could see the passing of a century. He, like Mother Earth, controlled much of the world everyone knew. Seeing him frozen made Liv realize how doomed they were. If he stayed that way, not only would Talon rule, ruining the world she worked to protect, but without Papa Creola, the world would quickly spiral into an abyss of destruction.

Stefan materialized behind Liv and she straightened, feeling his hand on her back. "Sorry, I was just worried," he said in her ear. "I trust you, though."

Liv turned to him, realizing he couldn't understand her better. She didn't want a partner who told her what to do. Who yelled at her when she did what she wanted. She needed someone beside her who complemented her. Stood strong beside her, supporting and believing in her—just as Stefan had done.

Liv nodded. "It's not a trap. They are through those doors." That felt true, as if she'd been here before.

"How do you know that?" Rory asked from behind her.

"Maybe because it's written right there." Rudolf pointed to an engraving above the door.

It read those who seek to save the ones I turn to stone must earn a token from each of the gorgon sisters. Ahead lie the traps of our souls. - Medusa"

"Not much of a poet, is old Medusa?" Rudolf asked.

"So one room must belong to Stheno," Trudy remarked contemplatively.

"And another to Euryale," Akio added. "They were both immortal."

"But what about Medusa?" Stefan asked.

"She can be killed," Rory stated. "But don't be deceived. She will be the hardest to defeat."

"Okay, we need those tokens," Liv decided at once. "We're going to split up." She pointed to the first room. "Akio and Trudy, take that door. Rory and Rudolf, you go into the second room. Stefan and I will take Medusa's."

Liv bounded in the direction of the first door, quickly realizing that no one was moving. She spun around, worried they'd all been turned to stone. They were simply blinking at her.

"What are you waiting for?" Liv asked them.

"I don't know," Rudolf answered. "Maybe a speech or something, fearless leader."

Liv sighed. "Seriously? We're running out of time. And Medusa could… No, scratch that, *is* somewhere around here waiting to make us look just like Papa Creola. Go into the door I assigned you and get the token."

No one budged.

Liv rolled her eyes and added, "Please."

Still they all simply blinked at her. "Fine," she stated. "Go forth and defeat the gorgon sisters. Progress cautiously, never looking anywhere without first glancing at a reflective surface. And get back here alive, because if anything happens to any of you, I'm going to be livid."

Rudolf laughed, clapping Rory on the back. "I don't know about you, but that was the fire I needed under my butt. Ready to go face a lady who probably hasn't had a date in a long, long time?"

Rory nodded. "Yes, let's do it."

Akio and Trudy saluted Liv. She was taken aback by the show of respect, but she accepted the gesture, watching them as they marched toward their door.

After the other two teams had disappeared, Liv turned to Stefan. "Are you ready for this?"

He grinned at her with a fierce expression in his eyes. "As someone wise once said to me, 'I don't think it matters much if I'm not.'"

# CHAPTER THIRTY-FOUR

Akio Takahashi was used to working alone. However, he was actually looking forward to working alongside Trudy DeVries.

He had a great fondness for seers since his grandmother Kazuko was once one. One of her prophecies had stated that a Warrior for the House would one day have her gift. Although Trudy had never told Akio she was an oracle, he had known it from the beginning, having recognized the same wisdom in her eyes that he'd seen in his grandmother's while growing up.

Akio also had great respect for Liv Beaufont. She had an instinct that his father stated couldn't be taught; it was inborn. She was braver than most and carried herself with a grace that spoke of her affection for life. There were few Akio would take orders from, but Liv was definitely one. When she had paired him with Trudy, he'd known it was the right call. He believed they would balance each other.

Cautiously, he slipped the blade of his sword Rakurai through the crack of the door, careful to keep his eyes on only it. The reflective surface showed a large room lit by torches. The smell of moss prickled his nose, and the sound of moving water greeted his ears.

He gave Trudy a quick glance over his shoulder. "I think it's clear."

She nodded down at him, being much taller than Akio.

Letting out a long breath, Akio kept his head down and his eyes on the stone floor as he entered the large room. It wasn't the way he had ever approached a fight. His father had taught him to keep his chin high and eyes searching when in battle, but facing one of the gorgon sisters or whatever was in this room required a different approach.

A splash of water echoed at his back. He tilted his sword, eyeing the blade. There was nothing. The width of the blade made it impractical as a reflective surface. Akio was about to summon a wall of water, as the elves had taught him to do, but Trudy interrupted him.

"That's not necessary," she said, turning to face the pool at their backs.

Akio didn't ask how she had known what he was about to do, or why it was unnecessary. Instead, he simply copied her movements, looking around the cavernous room. The murky water in front of them skipped as if a breeze had just passed over it. The pool was about half the size of an Olympic-sized swimming pool. It was too dark to see what was swimming below the surface, although Akio knew it had to be something large from the way the water swelled.

"How do we know Medusa won't materialize?" Akio asked in a whisper, continuing to scan the surface of the water.

"I know," Trudy said through clenched teeth, holding her heavy sword at the ready.

"Anything else you'd like to pass along?" Akio asked as a fin broke the top of the water. It disappeared at once.

"Yes, you should take that end," Trudy answered.

"Of the pool?" Akio questioned.

She shook her head as the largest sea monster Akio had ever seen shot out of the tank. A soul-crushing scream issued from its wide mouth and echoed through the room. The thing had several rows of teeth and a vengeful look in its black eyes. It was like a cross between a large snake and the Loch Ness monster.

The beast's back was covered in sharp spikes. On its front were two lateral fins that flailed, splashing water all over Trudy and Akio. It disappeared back under the water, creating large waves that rebounded across the pool, sending water over the sides and flooding the ground under their feet.

"You mean I should take the tail of the monster, then?" Akio questioned.

Trudy agreed with a nod. "I'll take the head. Don't underestimate the tail's range. It can reach much farther than you think."

"Meaning?" Akio dared to ask.

"That if you don't want a repeat of what I've seen, expect that there is no place in this room safe from this sea monster."

Akio nodded, again grateful to be alongside the seer. It appeared she'd already helped save his life.

# CHAPTER THIRTY-FIVE

R ory stopped Rudolf before they entered the door. "Do you have a weapon?"

The fae tapped the side of his head. "Yes, the most deadly one ever. My brain."

The giant rolled his eyes, realizing they were probably doomed. He had his magic, though, and he wanted to think that Rudolf could be helpful in a jam. He had survived for over half a century...somehow.

"Put down some ice, would you?" Rory asked, cracking the door to the second room but keeping his eyes directed away.

Rudolf sighed as if this were the smallest of tasks. He then pointed his finger through the opening beside the door, creating a thin layer of ice on the floor and wall just inside. "All done, my large friend."

Rory opened the door a bit more, staring down at the icy floor as Rudolf studied the sheet along the wall.

"All clear," the fae stated, pushing the door all the way open and stepping in. He immediately slipped on the ice, his feet sliding out from under him, sending him to his back. "I'm okay." He coughed on the words, not sounding okay at all.

"I'm not sure putting ice on the floor was such a good idea," Rory said, keeping his eyes on the wall of ice that reflected the room before them as he stepped over Rudolf. The reflection didn't show them much, just that Medusa wasn't standing there waiting to turn them to stone. Actually, Rory could have sworn that he saw shrubbery in the reflections, but he couldn't be sure.

Staring at the wall of ice, he offered his hand to Rudolf, helping the fae up from the floor. "Would you please create some more ice walls?"

Rudolf grabbed his chest, batting his eyes at Rory. "I'm not used to being talked to with such politeness. Usually, it's 'Ru, do this' or 'King, your pants are on backward.' Oh, and then there's, 'Sign all these forms so we can keep redheads out of the rooftop pools. Their pale skin is blinding the helicopter pilots.' Also, 'Your pants are on backward again, King.' There is never any requests or pleases. How nice it is to be respected."

"You don't seriously...never mind." Rory shook his head. "And yes, if you wouldn't mind helping out with the reflective surfaces, but only on the walls."

"Not at all," Rudolf stated, swirling his hand over his head. A cracking noise echoed through the room, like how water sounds when it freezes. It made Rory realize how large the room was. He shot a cautionary glance at the wall of ice in front of them, his eyes bouncing to the right as he cleared the distance, studying the two adjacent walls covered in ice that reflected each other.

When he was certain that the area in front of them was safe, he turned to face forward and brought his chin up.

Rudolf did the same.

They let out simultaneous noises of amazement. There, in front of them and seemingly stretching for miles, was a gigantic maze, its walls covered in ice.

# CHAPTER THIRTY-SIX

L iv used Athena's shield to check the space inside the door to the third room. She jumped when the mirrored surface caught an image, but relaxed when she realized it was Plato.

"The coast is clear," the lynx said, nodding her into the dark room.

Although surprised to hear him talk with Stefan at her back, she wasn't totally astonished. Plato had been different since losing his last life and then regaining another hundred.

Peeling the door back, Liv glanced around, then waved Stefan into the space.

"Oh, this is where you left your cat," the demon hunter said upon finding Plato just inside the dark space. It was a fairly plain room, mostly dark, save for two torches on the side of a flat, rectangular stone on the other side.

"Yes, he likes to hang around in weird places and pops up when I least expect him," Liv said, carefully scanning the area. "How do we know Medusa isn't going to simply materialize somewhere in here and turn us to stone for looking at her ugly face?"

"Well, keep insulting her in her home, and she might," Plato answered. "However, I don't think facing Medusa in here is part of the challenge."

Liv lowered her chin, staring directly at the lynx. "It sounds like you know what we're supposed to do. Why don't you share?"

"I promised the youngest of the gorgon sisters long ago that I wouldn't give away her secrets," Plato answered.

Liv's eyes widened. "You've met her?"

He shrugged. "I wouldn't really call it a meeting since we never came face to face."

"Ha-ha," Liv stated. "Do you really know the trick to this room?"

"I do, but I'm unable to share it with you," he answered.

Liv gave Stefan a look of annoyance. "Isn't that cute? I bet you wish you had a sidekick like mine."

"I'm good," he stated, his clear blue eyes running over the room.

Returning her attention to the lynx, Liv stuck her hands on her hips. "Seriously, you aren't going to tell us what do to here?"

"I can't," Plato answered. "I wish I could, but an ancient law keeps me from sharing the secrets of Medusa's temple."

Liv took a step toward the stone block at the back of the room that looked like an altar. "Can you tell me if I'm getting warmer or colder?"

"I can, but it will have nothing to do with your objectives," he stated. "It will simply be based on how close you are to the torches."

Liv slumped in defeat. "Fine, you're no help at all."

"Be careful how soon you dismiss me," Plato said, a warning in his voice.

Liv cast him a tentative glance over her shoulder as she turned to better study the room. There was a round disk on the ceiling over the block, and above that were words, which were hard to make out in the dimly lit room.

Lifting her hand, Liv released a fireball, sending it to glide past next to the words and illuminate the message.

The words read To get the token you desire, put what you love most into the fire.

Liv scratched her head. "That's weird. Are we supposed to burn nachos over those tiny torch flames?"

Stefan laughed. "I think that what we all love is different. For some of us, it might not be a pile of chips, but rather a person."

She smiled slyly at the man before her. "Well, maybe one day, you'll meet the right plate of nachos."

"Maybe," he agreed coyly. He studied the area around the riddle, his eyes speculatively resting on the symbol above it. "I wonder." Holding the bow up, he eyed it carefully before launching an arrow at the round symbol.

Sparks shot from it when the arrow struck and rained down, and as if lit by the small embers, a roaring fire shot up from the altar. The flames would have scorched anything on the slab.

Liv turned to Stefan, a tentative expression on her face. "I'm sorry about this, but I think I need to burn you alive to pass this test."

# CHAPTER THIRTY-SEVEN

Trudy DeVries was built like a man, with her wide shoulders and a thick torso. Because of her short blonde hair, from the back, she was often mistaken for a male. That had never bothered her, though. She knew that her role as a seer meant she encompassed both genders. She also knew that true happiness wasn't in the cards for her, not in this lifetime.

That wasn't because she'd seen her future in a vision, like when she had seen Akio getting pummeled by the spiky end of the sea monster's tail in her mind just prior to entering the room where they stood. She knew happiness wasn't something she'd truly find because that was the curse of an oracle. They might marry and have children, and most likely they'd live a long life, but happiness wasn't something easy to achieve when one could see the future. It was a true burden, and one Trudy shouldered with great reverence.

She had been direct with Akio about having seen his future because she trusted him, and she knew the Takahashi had protected seers. Kazuko, Akio's grandmother, had been one of the most influential of her time. However, her life had followed the path of most seers', bringing many enemies to her door until she was finally shut off from the world.

Even in modern times, seers were persecuted. It didn't seem as contradictory to Trudy as it should have that a world that held many magical races couldn't accept someone who could see the future. Her gift intimidated most. It scared them. Prophecies weren't something people tolerated, because they set the future in concrete. When people found out their fate, they were rarely relieved. Usually it carried with it a great burden, which was why Hester DeVries had been adamant that her sister Trudy not publicize the fact that she could see the future. They had protected it together, keeping it from anyone who would hunt her down or exploit her gift.

Trudy had broken that promise to her sister only a few times to tell others what she'd seen. This time she'd done it because if she didn't, Akio would be dead, and with him, one of the greatest Warriors to ever live. Although Trudy didn't feel good about admitting this information to Akio, she had been compelled to, pushed on by the passion of the battle.

Furthermore, Trudy believed his death would most likely result in her own, since it would take both warriors to defeat the large sea monster swimming before them, waiting for its time to strike.

The beast's long snout sprang over the side of the tank, its teeth chomping, making Trudy jump back as she swung her sword at the monster. That kept it back some, but she knew it was merely studying her, trying to figure out how she would respond.

She shot a glance down the other side of the tank, where Akio was diving and rolling out of the way of the long tail, which followed his movements even though it had no eyes. Watching Akio fight was like seeing an expert dancer with hypnotizing choreography. He moved before the tail did, anticipating each of its movements. The spike hammered into the ground, cracking it and raining debris down from overhead.

Trudy realized she'd only half been paying attention to the snapping jaws trying to reach her when teeth clipped her armor, shredding it instantly. Her outfit was made from dragonhide and should have been hard to penetrate. The sea monster's teeth were obviously diamond or something of similar sharpness.

Jumping back before the next assault, Trudy allowed herself to get too close to the tank. The monster's lateral fin knocked her back. She knew it was going to happen before it did. Akio's eyes connected with hers, horror in them as realization dawned.

She tried to keep her balance by swinging her arms, but it was no use. The momentum of the attack sent her into the tank and she sank deep into the murky water, holding her grandfather's sword.

# CHAPTER THIRTY-EIGHT

"Can you see over the walls?" Rudolf asked, jumping to try to peer over the tall frozen shrubbery in front of them. He could make out several rows in front of this one. Freezing the walls had given him a partial blueprint of the large room, but not enough information to help them to navigate through it. He knew that a maze of this sort was supposed to make the traveler lost for so long that their life ended from starvation or dehydration.

Thankfully, Rudolf could produce ice for thirst, but one couldn't live on ice alone. He'd tried once when he'd accidentally locked himself in an empty walk-in freezer. To his relief, the restaurant's owners had come to his rescue and let him out. It wasn't lost on him that he had incredible magical powers, yet he couldn't get himself out of a locked freezer. Such was the craziness of a magical life.

"Just barely," Rory answered. "But not enough to see the way through."

"Well, thankfully, I don't think we have to worry about

Medusa in here," Rudolf said, striding down the narrow corridor, the only way they could go until the first bend.

"Why is that?" Rory asked.

Rudolf turned, walking backward. "Because the maze is the challenge."

"How can you be so sure?" Rory trailed carefully after him.

He shrugged. "Experience. I bet the first room has a monster we have to slay. This one is the cerebral challenge. Thankfully Liv assigned us to it."

"Yea, thankfully," Rory said doubtfully.

"The last room will involve offering a sacrifice of some sort," Rudolf explained.

"Again, how do you know this?" Rory questioned.

"Oh, I spent a lot of time with the Greek gods back in the day," Rudolf stated.

"I didn't realize you were that old."

Rudolf shrugged. "Past life sort of stuff."

"Well, don't you think you could have said something about this to Liv beforehand?" Rory asked.

He shook his head. "I forgot until just now. Hard to keep up with everything all the time, but now I remember. There will be a maze ahead of us, as well as some mental challenges. Don't worry, though, my tall friend. I'll get us through."

"Sure, you will," the giant said, sounding unconvinced.

Rudolf rounded the first bend, finding two different routes they could take. "Okay, first things first, I'm going to need a boost."

"Boost?" Rory asked.

"Well, the walls were designed so that two men or

women standing on each other's shoulders wouldn't be able to see over the top to get through the maze—"

"Oh, no," Rory said, cutting him off.

"Oh, yes," Rudolf stated. "If I get on your shoulders, Mr. Giant, I should be able to see the path through the maze."

"Why do *you* have to be on *my* shoulders?" Rory questioned.

"Well, because I'm lighter and have practice being on the top of a pyramid," Rudolf stated. "I was once a cheer officer for the Rams."

Rory's eyelid twitched in annoyance. "Of course you were."

"Anyway, if you'll just cup your hands and give me a little boost, that would be great."

"You're not serious, are you?" Rory asked.

"You want to hear about serious, try spending a night with Achilles. That guy was a real heel!"

Rory didn't laugh along with Rudolf. Instead, he simply shook his head and threaded his fingers together. "Okay, fine. You can stand on my shoulders."

Holding onto the giant's shoulders, Rudolf put his boot into the foothold his friend made and stepped up.

"Ouch, you stepped on my ear," Rory complained as Rudolf tried to balance on his shoulders.

"Sorry. If they weren't so big…" Rudolf began, bracing himself on the giant as he surveyed the top of the maze. It was huge, going on for what seemed like miles. Without this advantage, they would starve before making it to the other side.

A bolt of fire shot at them from a dark corner. Rudolf caught sight of it just in time, diving off the giant's shoulders and rolling on the ground. Rory wasn't as quick and the fire grazed his head, singeing his hair.

"Ahhh!" he yelled, sticking his flaming head against the icy wall in front of him. It thawed the shrubbery immediately, causing it to drip into a puddle below.

"Yeah, small thing I forgot to mention," Rudolf said matter-of-factly.

"That when you cheat to get through the maze, there are repercussions?" Rory asked, not amused by the lesson.

"Well, the gods don't like cheaters, so they punish them," Rudolf explained. "But I did see that we take the first left, second right, and then another left."

"And then what?" Rory asked, his chin low and his eyes brimming with annoyance.

"And then it's time for me to jump up on your shoulders again." He waved Rory forward, encouraging him to follow.

"I'm not sure I want you on my shoulders again," the giant complained.

"Come on, Hercules," Rudolf encouraged. "You can do it!"

Rory shook his head. Rudolf could have sworn his tough exterior was cracking.

## CHAPTER THIRTY-NINE

"Liv Beaufont, is that your way of telling me you're in love with me?" Stefan asked.

The fire covering the altar had gone out, leaving them in mostly darkness again, but Liv's fireball still hovered beside the message.

"Yes, I think it is, but I'm also trying to tell you that I think according to Medusa's riddle, I need to sacrifice you in order to get through this room." She read the etched words aloud. "To get the token you desire, put what you love most into the fire." Turning to Plato, she gave him a questioning glare.

He simply nodded.

"Oh, well, it's been nice knowing you, Warrior Ludwig," Liv said, pointing to the altar and trying to cover her giggle.

"I'm waiting for the 'but,'" he answered, giving her a smug glare.

"I do love you, and I'll miss you, *but* Papa Creola's life is on the line. I might have feelings for you, but they aren't more important than the entirety of time. And then there's Talon. I think we both know he has to be ended before it's too late."

"Yes, but the thing is, I don't really want to die," Stefan stated.

Liv nodded. "And I don't want you to. Not at all. Actually, I'd rather lie down on that fiery slab myself, but I'm not sure that satisfies the test."

She glanced at Plato. He shook his head. "I can tell you that it has to be whoever you love most, Liv."

She turned back to Stefan, realizing she was playing a game with him that he'd later punish her for. "I'm sorry, Stef. You need to die, but I'll honor your memory."

"Are you serious?" Stefan asked, walking reluctantly toward the altar. "I mean, I get it, and I'll do it because I want Papa Creola freed, but let's briefly discuss another option."

Liv let him get to the altar before she winked at Plato. "I'm just grateful that you are willing to give up your life for this. It means a lot."

"Of course," Stefan said, pulling himself up and sitting on the altar like a child trying to get into a high chair. He didn't appear scared, only like he was bracing himself for what would happen next. It almost made Liv feel bad for the mean trick she was playing on him.

"Okay, cool," she stated. "Now go ahead and pop off that altar so that you can shoot that symbol again with your bow and arrow."

Stefan gave her an expression of confusion. "But who…"

She pointed at the lynx beside her. "I love you, Stefan. You have to know that by now. That was kind of a crummy way of telling you, but our lives aren't normal. But the one I love more than any other is this one. He's the one I have to sacrifice to pass." Liv pointed at Plato, who was sitting regally beside her.

"But…" Stefan didn't appear to know how to respond as he looked at Liv and Plato, still shocked by her admission. "I…"

Plato cut him off and flicked his tail. "She's right. I'm who she loves most."

"And you're just going to allow him to sacrifice himself for this?" Stefan asked.

Liv nodded, looking proudly at Plato. "It's what he wants to do, and I promised him that if such an occasion arose, he could take it."

"But he'll die," Stefan argued.

Liv simply shrugged. "Yeah. Oh, well."

He lowered his chin and regarded her from hooded eyes. "What's so special about your sidekick? I mean, I saw him do some cool stuff on the Matterhorn, but what else makes him unique?"

She shot Plato an affectionate expression. "He's super loyal."

"And?" Stefan continued.

"He's always there for me," she continued.

"What else have you yet to tell me about this creature?" Stefan asked.

"Like most cats, he's got more than one life," she stated.

Stefan let out a breath. "So you can sacrifice him, and everything will be okay?"

"Well, you're not the one who has to burn up, are you?" Plato gave him a rude stare.

"Keep in mind that Liv nearly burned up my heart by making me think she was okay with sacrificing me as her best friend."

She giggled. "Oh, come on. It was funny."

Stefan seemed to be trying to control the laughter simmering under the surface, but it burst through. "Yeah, fine. Well played, Warrior Beaufont."

Liv kneeled and picked up the black and white cat. "Are you sure about this? I know we said that if—"

"It's just one life, Liv. I have ninety-nine more."

"Oh, is that all?" Stefan rolled his eyes.

"He goes through them faster than I'd like," Liv told him.

"I would too if I was your sidekick," he retorted.

"Watch yourself, Ludwig, or I'll considering loving you more than the lynx," she stated.

He held up his hands. "No, no. I've got lots of bad habits that you haven't realized yet. I frown when I sleep, and I will treat you like you're always wrong and be combative for no reason. Oh, and I'll steal food off your plate when you're not looking."

She narrowed her eyes at him. "None of that's true."

Stefan smiled at her. "You're right. I'm a catch."

Liv shook her head at him, returning her focus to Plato in her arms. "Seriously, though. You are my favorite, and you don't have to do this."

"I appreciate you saying both of those things, but I do," he explained. "It's the only way to get the token, and without that, you won't unfreeze Papa Creola."

"But what if you hadn't entered this room with the love of your life?" Stefan asked. "Or conversely, if your sidekick didn't have the ability to materialize beside you?"

Liv and Plato both cast an annoyed glare at him.

"Then the task would have been different. It is based on who enters the chambers," Plato explained.

"Oh, so the other's rooms tasks were specifically designed for them, then?" Stefan asked, stroking his chin. "Very interesting."

The lynx looked up at Liv. "You sure about this one? I get that he's cute and all, but one glance from Medusa and you can look at him without all the lip."

Liv laughed. "Well, I guess there's something wrong with me, but I like his remarks."

"Suit yourself." Plato jumped out of her arms and onto the altar. "And don't worry about me, Liv. I want to do this. It will hurt worse than that one time I pulled your boyfriend out of the clutches of that demon who was hiding in a volcano, ready to suck out his soul."

"That was you?" Stefan asked in disbelief.

Liv glanced at Stefan over her shoulder. "He's a very odd creature."

He nodded. "He called me your boyfriend."

Liv dismissed him with a shake of her head and pointed to the crest over the altar. "And I'm calling you a different, lesser name unless you hit that target."

Stefan winked at her, holding his bow at the ready. "Thanks, Plato. You're pretty much the best ever."

Liv smiled at her best friend, sitting majestically and bravely on the altar before them. She took a step back. "You *are* the best, and I love you more than anything."

"Same to you," Plato said as Stefan shot the arrow.

Liv turned, unable to watch as the fire roared up, burning anything that was on the platform.

# CHAPTER FORTY

"Oh, my gods," Rudolf went on. He hadn't stopped talking since they'd started the trek through the maze. "Let me just tell you, Narcissus was always 'Me, me, me.' I couldn't get in a word edgewise. Can you imagine?"

Rory trudged onward. "Hardly."

"And then there was Sisyphus," Rudolf went on. "Was that guy a whiner! 'It's heavy. I'm tired. I have to do it *again?*'"

"I'm sure your impression is spot-on," Rory stated.

"Let me just tell you about Daedalus. That guy was so lost." Rudolf stopped abruptly after the third turn. "Looks like it's time for me to hike to the top of your shoulders again, Ro-Ro."

"It's Rory," he corrected. "And actually, your stories of the Greeks give me an idea."

"If you say I need to marry my cousin and start a war with my father, well, that was so last century," Rudolf stated. "I'm past all that immature behavior now."

Rory let out a breath. It wasn't that he didn't find

Rudolf endearing. Quite the opposite. There was a wisdom in the fae few could match, and the giant was having a hard time covering up his usual act of disdain. Liv was good about breaking through his tough exterior, but no one else. But Rudolf? Well, he was challenging Rory in ways he hadn't expected.

"No, your story about Daedalus got me thinking," Rory began. "In his story, he got trapped in the labyrinth he created. He and Icarus tried to fly out of it, but his son flew too close to the sun, hence the fire when we tried to cheat the maze."

"I'm following you, I'm following you," Rudolf said, encouraging Rory to continue. "But if I wasn't, how would you explain it, so I understood better?"

"Well, the problem with Daedalus was that he—"

"Didn't wear enough clothes?" Rudolf cut in.

Rory shook his head.

"Built a maze for a controlling dictator?" Rudolf suggested.

The giant cut his eyes to the side.

"Oh, is it that he tried to overcompensate with big wings?"

"No," Rory answered, surprised that a laugh slipped from his mouth. "It's that Daedalus overthought everything. The easiest solutions are always the best."

With a firm intention, Rory stomped his foot, making the ground under them vibrate. A crack started at his boot and shot through the maze, splitting the shrubbery walls in two, giving them an easy way to tell where they should be going. It wouldn't be as fast as looking over the top, but it would get them through without being shot at with fire.

Rudolf considered him with his mouth hanging wide open. "Rory Laurens, you're an absolute genius. You totally remind me of Athena, except that she had a better rack and this thing she could do with a cherry stem."

Whether it was because Rory was relieved there was a path to the exit or because Rudolf had worn him down, he let out a loud laugh. "Come on, King, let's get out of here."

"Sure thing," Rudolf said, skipping next to him. "I guess I could have also likened you to Poseidon, except that's a bad idea in Medusa's temple since she hated him and all."

CHAPTER FORTY-ONE

"No!" Akio yelled, trying his best to send a spell at Trudy that would pull her back over the side of the tank. His own battle with the relentless tail made that impossible. The warrior was gone, having been swept over the rim of the tank.

The tail and head of the monster disappeared under the water, same as Trudy.

*That couldn't be good,* Akio thought as he ran to where she'd fallen into the pool. Large bubbles rose up to the surface and he could just make out a swirling white shape, but there was no sign of Trudy.

She was the reason he was still alive. Akio would have been taken out by the monster's tail, underestimating its range if it weren't for Trudy. And now she was the one in danger. He had to do something. However, it was impossible to fight the creature while it was under the surface of the water. That was why he decided it was time to bring the monster up.

He held out his free hand and muttered an incantation that

immediately sucked the power from his core. This was a risk. He was sorry to do this to Trudy, but he had to do whatever it took to save her, even if it meant slightly boiling her alive.

---

Trudy stayed as still as she could manage, realizing that the monster had limited vision. Like many sea animals, it could sense movement and vibrations. In the dark water it called home, its sight was restricted.

She held her breath, knowing she had a limited time before her air ran out. But if she tried to swim back up right then, the monster would have her eaten before she was halfway to the surface. Instead, she cemented her back against the wall of the tank, feeling the algae dance across her head and neck.

The head of the monster nearly made her open her mouth from fright, and she let out all her air and swallowed gallons of water. It came out of the darkness, nearly ramming into her. Trudy remained stone-still though, her eyes wide, watching as the beast spun to the side just before colliding with her. Its body moved like a snake, slithering past her, the spiked tail swishing back and forth.

Trudy held tight to the sword, slowly trying to move it in front of her.

The monster whipped around, its black eyes running over her as it opened its mouth wide, its razor-sharp diamond teeth like glowing lights in the dark water. It rushed in her direction. It knew her location. She was screwed. The frigid water instantly changed, feeling like

Trudy had taken a dip in a bubbling hot tub instead of a cold, salty tank.

The monster screamed under the water, making a sound that vibrated Trudy's teeth. She was just about to spring after the beast, knowing she was out of options, when it changed course, shooting straight toward the surface of the water.

---

The water in the tank began to bubble as the temperature grew hotter. Akio knew that sea creatures, especially ones like this, preferred cold water.

Trudy had been under for almost a minute. He didn't have long. Akio needed this to work. He watched anxiously as steam rose off the surface of rapidly boiling water. Not only did he need to get Trudy out of the tank, but he also couldn't keep heating the massive pool. The feat had already seriously depleted his magical reserves.

Akio was about to abandon this plan and dive into the tank after Trudy when a shriek filled the air as the giant sea monster sprang up from the center of the tank head-first. It shot so high up that its pointy snout knocked into the high ceiling, rocking the entire room. Stones rained down, making Akio dart to the side several times while covering his head.

The sea monster continued to wail, flailing like a bucking bull. Akio was searching the tank for signs of Trudy when something on the side of the creature caught his attention. Sitting behind one of the spiny fins with her legs straddling the beast was Trudy DeVries, her sword over her head, the point facing downward.

Akio realized what she was going to do, and knew that he had to save her after the fact. She might be able to attack the monster, but she wouldn't survive it unless he helped. Akio lifted his hand as more stones rained down from overhead, but that didn't break his focus as he used the last of his reserves to speak an enchantment.

Trudy plunged her sword deep into the sea monster, making blood spray out in all directions. The creature screamed louder than ever and its tail flew up, smashing into the side of the tank. Trudy twisted her sword with a jerk, making the wound bigger.

The monster writhed, but Trudy didn't relent. Instead, she pulled her sword out and appeared ready to stab it again. Blood shot out of the gaping hole in the side of the beast. A large stone fell from overhead, smashing onto the tail whipping around on the side of the pool and pinning it.

Both hands on the sword, Trudy swung it, slicing all the way through the monster and severing its head from the rest of its body.

If fell back into the pool with a huge splash, polluting the water with red. The rest of the monster swayed. Trudy still held tight to it with her legs but appeared ready to topple backward. Like a sinking ship, the sea monster's body was about to slam onto the surface of the water, bringing with it the rider who had slain it.

Akio sped up the words of his spell, holding his hand out. As the monster's body plunged toward the bloody water, he yanked his hand to the side. Trudy's body and sword copied his movements, yanked off the creature as she flew across the pool and slammed into the wall beside Akio.

She slid down the stone wall, covering her head against the crumbling ceiling. The room was going to cave in. They had to get out.

Akio sped over to her and helped her up. He noticed that she was bloody in many places, either from wounds she'd sustained while riding the spiky beast or from the monster's blood. She was limping, but he was able to drag her to the door as a large boulder fell, sending bits of rock and dust at their back.

"Thanks for rescuing me back there," Trudy said between breaths as she lumbered forward.

"Same to you," Akio said, turning back to the crumbling room, noticing that the pool appeared now like an angry sea, ready to capsize a boat.

They'd slain the beast, but where was the token?

Then he noticed that among the rock and water, there was something shiny lying ten yards away.

Making an impromptu decision, he thrust Trudy toward the arch of the doorframe as he dove for the coin. He rolled straight into a roundoff, followed by several backflips, trying his best to navigate the obstacles as the ceiling continued to crumble. He halted abruptly, kneeling when he was on top of the coin. Swiftly he grabbed it and tossed it to Trudy. She caught it as the ceiling caved in, covering Akio Takahashi in stone.

CHAPTER FORTY-TWO

Relief filled Liv's being when Plato appeared on the other side of the door in the main room. She was about to say something that bordered on sentimental when Rudolf and Rory thundered through the second door, the fae falling onto the giant as they rolled.

Liv rushed over to them, worried that they were hurt, but found both of them laughing like they'd simply been thrust out of a funhouse. "Are you okay?" she asked the pair, wondering if they had been put under a laughing spell. It sounded like a good way to go, but she'd heard it was incredibly torturous to laugh with no way of stopping. Starvation and dehydration followed quickly, making for a horrible end. The person continued to laugh like their demise was funny.

Rudolf pushed off Rory, then held a hand out to help the giant up. Rory shook his head, regaining his usually calm nature.

"We're fine, Liv," Rory answered, holding out his large hand, a shiny token sitting in the palm. "We got you this."

Liv smiled, taking it from the giant. "Thank you. Great work."

"And you?" Rory asked, his eyes sliding to Stefan behind her and Plato beside him.

She opened her other hand to reveal the coin with Medusa's portrait on it that she'd recovered after Plato had sacrificed himself. She still couldn't get the smell of burning flesh out of her mind. "Yes, we got the token, thanks to the bravery of someone I love very much."

"The most," Plato corrected, giving Stefan a smug expression.

"Still, she loves me," the demon hunter said. "She can't take it back. What one says in battle is true and binding."

Liv shook her head, giddy about surviving thus far.

A cloud of dust and rock shot from the first door as it opened. Trudy rushed through, diving to the floor and covering her head. The door shut behind her immediately.

"Trudy?" Liv asked cautiously.

The other Warrior lifted her head, her face covered in blood and dirt. She had never seen her appear more battered.

"Where is Akio?" Liv asked, but upon looking into Trudy's eyes, she knew the answer.

Tears welled and she shook her head, gasping like the oxygen was being sucked from her chest and replaced by pain. "Noooo," Liv said, not wanting to believe it.

"I'm sorry," Trudy said, standing. "I tried to save him. I did. But the thing is, you can't prevent someone's death, I've found. When it's their time, even if you warn them, the Reaper will just find another way to end their life."

The seer extended her hand. Liv copied the movement, holding her palm under Trudy's. She opened her fingers and the final token dropped into Liv's hand, clattering next to the others.

They had retrieved all three of Medusa's tokens.

# CHAPTER FORTY-THREE

L iv turned to the stone statue of Papa Creola,
surprised to find it unmoving. She had expected to
recover the tokens. Looking at her friends assembled on
the other side of the statue, she shook her head.

"I don't understand," she stated.

At her back, she felt a hot wind. A hiss. Knowing
exactly what she was missing, she dropped to the marble
floor as she yelled, "Look away!"

She heard her friends all swiftly pivot and hoped none
had seen the creature staring at her.

"So, you've come to battle me," a voice full of hisses and
scorn called from behind Liv.

She rose, noticing that Rudolf had quickly created a
sheet of ice in front of him and Rory that reflected the
creature behind her. Medusa wasn't ugly like she'd
thought. She wasn't the typical American girl next door,
either. This woman was a more exotic type, with her scaly
bronze skin and long hair made up of vicious cobras.

Medusa was wearing a sleeveless gown that flowed

with the same grace as the snakes that hovered above her head, but more entrancing than that was the way her eyes held this penetrating gaze that almost made Liv want to turn around so she could see them directly. She resisted the urge, realizing that was part of the treachery.

"I've come to free Father Time," Liv said, her back straight, looking at the image that hovered behind her in the reflection on the sheet of ice.

Medusa laughed, shaking the ground under their feet. "And you've earned the right to free him by getting the tokens. That has granted you the opportunity to battle me. Congratulations, Warrior Beaufont. I haven't had a good fight in ages."

And she's lost to no one, Liv guessed, watching as beside Rudolf, Trudy held up her large sword in front of her. It provided a view of Medusa from the left. Rudolf and Rory had the front covered.

Realizing exactly how this battle had to go down, Liv yelled to Stefan, "Hey, at your feet." She threw Athena's shield at the floor, and it skidded just in front of Stefan's boots.

He picked it up, holding it so she could see Medusa on the right. Now they had every angle covered, but the problem was that Liv needed to turn to face her enemy.

"I'm all too happy to battle you, Medusa," Liv said, yanking a piece of fabric from her trusty black cape. She winked at her friends, who could see her in the reflection of their sword, ice, or shield.

"And when I defeat you and your friends," Medusa began, "you'll become stone, giving me the power I need to escape this place where I've been imprisoned for too long."

Liv doubled over the piece of fabric until she was sure she couldn't see through it and wrapped it around her eyes, tying it tightly at the back of her head. "And when I win, you'll release Father Time and let us all go."

Medusa's laughter was lacking any joy. "Well, it sounds like we've struck a deal. I'll let you go *if* you win."

Liv pulled Bellator from its sheath and turned to face the woman who was the stuff of nightmares.

## CHAPTER FORTY-FOUR

L iv's friends didn't need her to instruct them on their next jobs. They all knew the plan once she had blind-folded herself. They were now her eyes. She felt Bellator pulse in her hands, and knew it too would help direct her.

Defeating Medusa would be about trusting her friends and relying on her weapon in a way she'd never done before, just as Akio had taught her. The thought of him didn't weaken her. Instead, she felt his spirit swell in her heart, cheering her on from the Beyond.

In order to free Papa Creola, Liv would have to put her faith into the ones she'd grown to love like family. Trust was the true Warrior's test. And when one passed it, they earned more than riches and fame. They earned love—the best gift of all.

"She's on your right," Trudy said as Liv held Bellator, her feet steady but her breath short.

Liv turned, somehow feeling the movement of the snakes as they struck and hissed on Medusa's head.

She swung Bellator, sending the blade all the way

around from right to left but coming up short. She stayed in a crouch, waiting for the next command from her team.

"She has pulled two blades," Stefan stated.

Liv nodded in reply.

"And she's wearing a super-hot dress," Rudolf stated. "That slit goes alllllll the way up."

Strangely, Liv was glad for the break in the tension. It was what Rudolf was good at. Better than all the rest.

"At your left hip!" Rory yelled.

Liv spun in that direction and thrust out her boot, connecting with something and pushing it down.

A shriek of offense spilled from Medusa's mouth.

"Good one," Rudolf stated. "You knocked Crazy-Head on her backside. That will teach you to mess with my friend."

"Try not to provoke her," Liv said, feeling breathless as she swung Bellator back and forth, hoping to simply catch Medusa by luck. It was very unsettling to not be able to see in battle, the time she relied on her eyes the most. But right then, relying on her friends was more important.

"Liv, she's crouching right in front of you," Trudy stated.

She brought Bellator overhead and then down, but it didn't slice through flesh. Instead, it sunk into the marble floor. Liv tried to pull it up, but the blade was stuck.

"On your left," Rory stated.

Liv didn't know what to do without her weapon. She ducked and felt something dive over her head.

"On your—"

A blade sank into Liv's calf as she tried to pull Bellator from the marble. She screamed and yanked up her foot, then threw her leg back in a donkey kick. She felt the heel of her boot connect with something, thrusting it backward.

"On your right," Rudolf stated. "That was what I was going to say, but it's over and done with now. We're moving on."

There was a collective yell, but no one said anything specific, so when something like an elbow thrust into her torso, Liv fell into the statue of Papa Creola. She rolled immediately, jumping to her feet. Several more times, her team told her where to dart or where Medusa was.

Continuously, she felt her hand drawn to Bellator, but every time she tried to pull the blade from its place, her legs were swept out from underneath her.

Medusa struck her with her small, sharp blades. Liv dodged, moving blind, just trying to get out from under the attacks.

"She's at your back," Trudy yelled.

Liv ducked, but nothing happened. Then she swung around and caught something by the waist. She didn't know if Trudy had seen the attack in real-time or in the future, but Liv finally felt like she had the advantage as she held onto Medusa's body. But then she didn't know what to do with her.

When the small blade sank into her forearm, she released the beast, clapping her hand to the wound.

Liv felt Bellator in front of her and knew that was the only way to end this. No matter where she was in the temple, she could find Bellator blindfolded.

Dropping her hands to the hilt, she tried again to pull it out. She yanked, but it was stuck in the marble.

"Liv!" Rory yelled, making her tense.

"Don't worry about it!" Stefan retorted, and Liv heard the whizz of an arrow as it buzzed over her shoulder, hitting something.

Medusa yelled.

Liv tried to pull out Bellator once more, and this time the blade came free.

"She's right in front of you!" her friends yelled in unison.

Liv brought Bellator up and around in a swift movement, not hesitating as the blade met flesh. She felt it slice cleanly through the neck of the beast, and an instant later, the sound of something squishy hitting the marble greeted Liv's ears.

Her friends rejoiced, and, excited, Liv pulled off the blindfold, turning to the statue of Papa Creola, careful to keep her eyes off the head at her feet.

Like a snowman defrosting back into a real person, Papa Creola's features shifted from gray stone to full of color once more. It seemed like a century since Liv had stared at the ruby-red cheeks or round nose of the man before her. She nearly ran forward to hug him when he began to finally move but remembered that he'd probably kill her if she did that.

Instead, she pulled her cape off and draped it over Medusa's head to ensure no one else would be petrified.

"Papa Creola, you're back," Liv said, relief in her voice.

The ground under them shook and the gnome shot her a worried expression. "Not quite."

Over their heads, a duet of female voices sang, "She'll let you go *if* you win. But we won't."

Papa Creola shook his head, gathering his strength.

"The Gorgon sisters don't quit." He held out his short arms. "Come in close, everyone."

The group rushed forward, all trying to cram into the space around Papa Creola as the building shook as if it were about to sink into the ocean. The world shifted into a cacophony of bright colors as they swirled and swished, winged beasts clawing at them. One of the sisters tried to grab Bellator, but Liv tugged it back as they flew.

She heard a loud cackle in her ears but also felt the magic of a giant, a fae, and magicians, and Liv knew that she could rest. Closing her eyes, Liv relaxed as Papa Creola brought them from the place he'd been trapped to one where they'd be safe—for a little while, at least.

# CHAPTER FORTY-FIVE

L iv awoke, looking up at the ceiling of the Fantastical Armory, suddenly filled with the same foreboding she'd had the last time, when Plato had died.

She bolted to a sitting position, gasping.

Stefan was immediately in front of her, and he ran his hands over her face. "Hey. You were injured a lot by Medusa's blades. We'll get you healed."

"She'll survive," Trudy called from somewhere close by.

Stefan shook his head, looking to the right. "Talk about a spoiler alert."

Liv tried to get up, but it took her a minute. With Stefan's help, she got to her feet. Right in front of her was a man she'd sorely missed.

Papa Creola stood before her, with Subner, his assistant, beside him. Before Liv could say a word, both Father Time and the man he called his best bowed low, honoring Liv Beaufont.

She didn't know what to say, so she simply waited until

they rose back up, since they weren't that far from the ground to begin with.

"Warrior Beaufont," Papa Creola began, "you rescued me."

She gestured, indicating Rory, Rudolf, Trudy, Plato, and Stefan. "We all did. And another friend who is no longer with us but was the best fighter I have ever known."

"Someone who didn't hesitate to go back, because that was what had to be done," Trudy said, her voice tight.

Papa Creola looked around at the group. "Yes, Akio Takahashi was a great Warrior, and his memory will live on. I'll ensure that. But I was put away for a very specific reason by an evil who has eluded me for quite some time."

"Talon Sinclair," Liv said.

Papa Creola nodded. "You're weak. You need time to recover."

Liv shook her head. "No, I'm fine. And we—"

"Oh, wow!" Rudolf exclaimed, cutting them off as he stared around the shop. "This place holds such fond memories."

Papa Creola turned, giving the fae a measured glare. "Touch anything, and I'll have your children as my slaves for the rest of time."

Instead of looking as scared as he should have, Rudolf's eyes grew wide. "Children? I'm having children! I wonder who is having them?"

"Maybe Serena?" Rory suggested.

Rudolf shrugged. "Maybe. Hard to tell. She's the love of my life, but I've been around the block, if you know what I mean."

Liv rolled her eyes. "I think we all know what you

mean." She stepped forward, her injured calf yelling at her. "Papa Creola, Talon needs to be stopped. That was one of the many reasons we brought you back. But just so you know, no matter, I'll always bring you back."

He winked at her. "Then hold onto the package, and leave Talon to me."

"The hell I will. If you're taking him down, I'll be right by your side," Liv said, stepping up beside the little man.

He cast a glance over his shoulder and nodded. "Very well. Warrior Beaufont can join me and any of her friends who risked their lives to bring me back. But know that this won't be like facing Medusa. Talon is a new evil, one that even I can't anticipate how to take down yet."

Stefan stepped up next to Liv. "I'll be there, no matter what the danger."

Rory actually smiled. "And I. Wherever Liv is, whatever she needs, I'll be there."

Trudy nodded as well. "I don't know how to defeat the God Magician either, but I will wield my sword against him."

"You can start by not calling him that," Papa Creola stated. "He created that title to give him power he's undeserving of. There is power in words. Call him Talon. Call him despicable. But do not call him anything that grants him power. He is no god."

"How about 'butthead?'" Rudolf offered, playing with something on the counter.

"King Rudolf?" Papa Creola yelled, startling everyone.

Rudolf turned. "Fine. I'll go on the mission with you all. I'll be in charge of donuts."

Liv scowled at the fae and he sputtered out a cough, covering his blunder.

"I-I-I meant," Rudolf stuttered. "Donut…do not underestimate my loyalty to this mission. I do not let anyone come between my friends and me."

Liv turned to Papa Creola. "Lead us, and we will follow. And whatever you need to defeat Talon, whether it be my strength or Rudolf's intelligence, you have it."

The gnome smiled at her. "Thankfully I don't have to rely on the latter, but I'm grateful to have your assistance, Warrior Beaufont."

## CHAPTER FORTY-SIX

The phone rang and rang in Liv's ear. The expression on Stefan's face as he stood across from her with his own phone pinned to his head didn't make her confident he'd gotten an answer.

"Any luck?" she asked as Trudy strode back into the Fantastical Armory wearing clean armor once more. Subner had tended her wounds, as well as Liv's.

Trudy shook her head. "No. I have a summoning stone for her, but it's not working."

That silenced everyone in the shop. Rudolf, who had been discussing tactics with Rory, glanced up. Liv had a summoning stone for him, and no matter where he was in the world, or what he was doing, it would pull her to him, no matter what.

"What can that mean?" Liv asked, looking around at her friends.

"It means she's dead," Trudy said, her voice cold, although the emotion was written plainly on her face.

"Not necessarily," Subner argued. "If she's not

summoned using the stone, that means something very powerful could be holding her captive."

Liv glanced at Stefan. "Any luck?"

She knew it was silly to ask the question. She would have known if he'd gotten hold of Raina. He shook his head.

"Clark isn't answering either," Liv stated. The Councilors were to go back to the House and play their parts, making Talon think they were doing everything he'd asked. But something must have gone terribly wrong.

"We have to get to the House," Stefan said, the same worry in his eyes as Liv felt vibrating in her chest.

"Okay, I'm ready," Liv said, grabbing one of the peanut butter chocolate cookies Subner had set out for them, along with a wide array of rich pastries and fresh juices. Liv hadn't felt like eating but knew that her magical reserves needed it.

"Not quite yet," Subner stated, holding up a finger. "You'll need to wait for Papa Creola. He's getting ready."

"Like, he's putting on his gnome catsuit for battle?" Rudolf asked.

Liv shot him a contemptuous glare.

He threw up his hands. "Oh, fine. No jokes. Liv makes jokes when stress is high and loved ones are in danger, but when I do it, it's uncouth."

"Pretty much," Stefan stated, starting to pace.

"While you wait, I want to upgrade your weapons," Subner stated, holding out his short hands to Trudy. "Your sword, Warrior DeVries."

When Trudy looked at Liv tentatively, she said, "Go ahead. He already upgraded mine so that it can open locks."

"And serve as a conduit to the founders while fighting an enemy," Subner imparted as he ran his hands over Trudy's sword.

Liv blinked at him. "You're the reason that Bellator... Why didn't you tell me?"

"I'm telling you now," he said simply, extending a hand to Stefan with an expectant expression on his face. "I'm done with the sword. Now I'll take your bow, Warrior Ludwig."

"What will my sword do now?" Trudy asked, picking her weapon back up.

"It won't do anything. That's up to you," Subner replied. "When used properly, it will slice through things that are ethereal that it would have passed straight through before."

"Why would she need to have that capability?" Stefan asked, watching as the gnome ran his hands over the bow, making it glow for a moment.

Subner gave him an impatient stare. "Fighting that which we can see is much easier than fighting that which we can't."

Liv slightly shrugged at Stefan, realizing she was completely used to Subner's cold and riddle-like manner and hardly even questioned it at this point.

"And my bow?" Stefan asked.

"It will do the same things as Warrior DeVries' sword, as well as home in on targets," the gnome explained.

"Why does it sounds like you're preparing them to fight etheric creatures?" Rory asked.

"Because if something is keeping Councilor DeVries from being summoned, then it makes the most sense that she's been possessed." Subner strode for the back, turning when he was next to the door to Papa Creola's basement office, which lay several stories below them.

"What?" Trudy asked. "Are you sure?"

Subner shook his head. "No, not at all. There are many other plausible scenarios, but knowing what I do about Talon and the House, I think that is the best possibility."

"If they have those things for their weapons, should you modify Bellator?" Liv asked.

"No," Subner answered. "It was done when I made the first upgrade."

Unable to stop herself, Liv rolled her eyes. "Oh, you and your surprises."

"Besides," Papa Creola said, materializing in the doorway, looking exactly the same as usual, sans catsuit, "you have fireball magic. That works well for many different types of evil creatures. Never forget that."

Liv nodded, thinking that must be of great importance if Papa Creola was mentioning it now.

He stepped forward, studying the group around him. "You've notified the other Warriors to meet us at the House?"

"Yes," Liv answered. "But no one else, as you requested."

"Very good," Papa Creola stated. "This is a family matter between one of the first royals and the House. I think it is fitting that besides me, the fae, and the giant, the Warriors be in charge of ridding their House of this infestation."

# CHAPTER FORTY-SEVEN

"Holy hell, this can't be good," Rudolf said when they stepped through the portal to Santa Monica in front of the palm reading shop.

"Hell by definition can't be holy," Papa Creola corrected.

"It was sort of an expression, Pops." Rudolf pointed. "Was it forecast that it would be partly cloudy with a chance of an apocalypse today?"

A round, almost black cloud hung directly over the two-story palm-reading shop that was the entrance to the House of Fourteen. The windows of the shop were broken, and half of the roof was missing. Strange black vines were crawling up the sides of the building, which was badly cracked in places.

Mortals who passed the group on the boardwalk were well aware of the danger, giving the building a wide berth as they strode by and eyeing the foreboding cloud.

Liv's heart beat fast in her chest, thinking of Clark trapped somewhere inside the House. She hoped he was merely trapped; she couldn't consider any other possibility. And then there were John and the rest of the Mortal Seven, who were locked in comas, their chimeras also knocked out. Time wasn't just of the essence, it was running out.

Lifting her hand the same way she always did to be granted access to the House, Liv paused and turned to face Papa Creola. "I know you can, but will Rudolf and Rory be able to enter the House since they aren't Royals?"

"I believe that anyone and anything can enter now," Papa Creola answered, striding past her and pushing the door open. Blackness swallowed the gnome as a whirl of dust swept from the shop door.

Turning to Stefan, Liv gave him a careful expression.

"We'll face this together," he said, offering her a soft smile that made her feel marginally better.

Nodding, Liv stepped into the House of Fourteen, realizing that after that day, nothing in the magical world would ever be the same. The battle that would ensue was going to define the future. The side that won would write the history books. They would create the laws. They would control the magical world, which plainly meant that they'd control the world at large.

# CHAPTER FORTY-EIGHT

Nothing Liv had seen up until that point could have prepared her for the sight inside the House of Fourteen. Before, the entryway and corridor had appeared like a condemned house, broken from neglect and abuse. They now looked more like a murder scene.

Liv's boots crunched on bones of small animals as she stepped up next to Papa Creola, who was surveying the area before them. Broken glass littered the floor and shards were stuck into the wall, blood seeping from the punctures as if the House was bleeding.

"It *is* bleeding," Papa Creola said as if he'd read Liv's thoughts.

Accustomed to not having much privacy in her own head anymore, she didn't flinch from the invasion. "The House?"

He nodded as the rest of the group, now including Emilio and Maria, filed in behind them, many of them covering their noses against the smell of rot swirling on the icy breeze that sailed down the corridor. "It is alive, as you know, built with the magic and blood of the founders. It appears that Talon is battling the House, which obviously doesn't want him to control it. He would rather destroy one of the most incredible displays of magic in history than lose."

Black vines covered in long thorns snaked over the walls in the corridor, covering the words of the founders— the ones that spoke of doom. Liv could barely make out one or two symbols since the fast-moving vines were knitting together over everything.

Papa Creola turned to the group. "King Rudolf Sweetwater and Rory Laurens, you are to fight the corruption spreading here, trying to take over the House. The entryway has always been one of the most powerful parts of this structure because it funnels the power into the three parts."

"Body, mind, and spirit," Liv said in a hushed voice, not sure how she knew that.

"Yes," Papa Creola affirmed. "The body of the house is the residential wing, where I fear the councilors are being held. The Black Void has always been the mind of the House, a place we once thought was clean and a refuge, but know now has been corrupted for a long, long time."

"What's there now?" Trudy asked. "Is that where Talon is hiding?"

"He is no longer hiding," Papa Creola answered, turning to the side and looking at the floor next to him. "And as you expected, the House has lost its mind. Without it, there is no saving this place."

Liv wondered who Papa Creola was talking to, but when Plato materialized, she realized she should have known. It had been the lynx who had guessed that the Black Void hadn't disappeared, it has simply spread. Just as negative thoughts take over one's body and spirit, the corruption Talon had done to the mind of the House was destroying it at the foundation.

"Can you do what needs to be done?" Papa Creola asked Plato.

The lynx simply nodded, his eyes moving to Liv, a strange boldness in his gaze.

"The Chamber of the Tree is the spirit of the House, right?" Stefan asked.

"Yes, which is where the Mortal Seven are trapped in comas or whatever Talon did to them," Liv stated.

"And it's where they will remain until this war is won or lost by us because it has always been mortals who held the true spirit of magic." Papa Creola turned back to the corridor, a serious expression on his usually cheerful face. "Talon can't take them out of the Chamber until he's destroyed more of the House, which is why you must all work fast. Otherwise, my efforts to battle Talon will be for nothing."

"But…" Liv began as the gnome stepped forward.

He looked at her expectantly. "Yes, Warrior Beaufont?"

"I want to help you," she said, knowing this battle was more than personal for her.

He nodded. "And you will. Find your brother first." With that last order, the father of time disappeared.

# CHAPTER FORTY-NINE

The five warriors moved up the stairs of the residential wing, two in front and three in the back, their eyes scanning for threats. Large cracks ran down the staircase, through which a howling wind spiraled into the space.

Screams echoed down each corridor as they passed a landing, but they continued upward. Liv led the team, Bellator showing her the way. Black mold quickly grew up the walls as they progressed as if spurred by their ascension.

"How do you know where you're going?" Emilio asked as they passed the third floor.

"I can feel it," Liv whispered, seeing something dark dancing on the landing ahead. "Get ready."

When they came to it, Liv halted, petrified by the sight before her. It was simply a dark shadow, but that wasn't what filled her with such terror. It was the feeling the force possessed.

An arrow whizzed by her, striking the dark figure and

making it burst into light. Liv shielded her head from the sparks that hit the floors, scorching them before going out.

"What was that?" Maria asked.

"Specters," Trudy answered. "They spread like cancer in the body, taking over each organ and shutting it down."

"Or in this case," Stefan related, "they take over our council, effectively shutting down the House."

Bellator pulsed twice in Liv's hands when they reached the next landing. "Two councilors are on this floor."

"Again, how do you know that?" Emilio asked.

She nodded at her sword. "Akio taught me how to use my weapon as a compass."

"Then you must have taken his instructions quite seriously," Trudy observed, "because that is not something one easily learns."

Liv nodded, her fondness for her combat instructor aching in her being. Now wasn't the time to grieve, though. There would be time for that later.

"Emilio and Maria," Liv ordered, "take this floor."

The two warriors nodded, charging carefully toward the dark hallways and disappearing at once, swallowed by shadows.

The three remaining warriors proceeded up the stairs, where the screams and piercing winds grew in intensity.

CHAPTER FIFTY

"How are we supposed to fix this?" Rudolf asked, grimacing at the bloodstained walls.

"We need to cut it off from the rest of the House," Rory guessed. There was no way to know for sure, but Papa Creola was right that this was the funnel of energy to the House. Close off the bottleneck, and the energy couldn't spread to the residential wing, Black Void, and Chamber of the Tree.

"And how do we do that?" Rudolf questioned.

"Well, I think we start with frost," Rory stated, again not entirely sure. "That's how winter starts. Everything must die in order to come back anew."

"Easy-peasy." Rudolf held out his hands, but unlike when they were in Medusa's temple, ice didn't spray from his fingers to cover his target. He peered at his hands like they were broken. "That's odd. Do you think I can't do anything because I'm in the House?"

"No, I think you're being blocked by the corruption,

which doesn't want to be cut off because it wants to continue to spread."

Rudolf scratched his head. "Well, you've got earth magic. Will that do us any good?"

"Not unless you want me to bring the entire structure down," Rory answered.

"Yeah, the thing is that I don't," Rudolf said with a laugh.

The giant peered at the black vines, which were unlike anything he'd ever seen. Usually organic matter registered for Rory in a different way than other elements, triggering his magic and fueling it. But these vines were like oil, bubbling up from the earth, offering nothing but the spread of pollution and greed.

"If only you had some weed-killer," Rudolf remarked as the vines grew, making a gross scratching sound as they covered more of the walls and ceiling.

Taken aback by the epiphany, Rory threw his large hand back into Rudolf's chest, nearly knocking him over. "That's it. You're a genius."

The fae's face transformed with shock. "I knew the day would come when I heard those words. Why am I a genius?"

"Hatred is a fast-growing weed," Rory said slowly, the words coming to him one at a time as he worked out the theory in his head. "Talon loathes nothing more than the other races, and that was why he tried to cut the House off from the rest of the world. But what if we fought his hate with the only thing that can truly kill it?"

"Guns?" Rudolf guessed. "I'm not sure that's a good

idea. I'm anti-guns after being shot by a musket when I was in the Revolutionary War."

"You were… Never mind," Rory said, waving him off. "And no, not guns. The opposite. Love. Talon expects his hatred to be battled. He expects us to use force or elemental magic. But what a monster like him hasn't guarded his force of destruction against is a noncombatant form of attack. If we—"

"Make love, not war, then the vines won't know how to defend against it," the fae interrupted, his voice full of excitement.

"Yes, although I hope you realize that making love is figurative in this case," Rory stated.

Rudolf winked at him. "Hey, this isn't the sixties anymore. I don't swing that way. So what do we do?"

Rory let out a long, hot breath. "One of the most difficult things for any race to do: simply love. Send it everywhere, no matter the fear you feel in your heart. If you experience a threat or worry, then it's that much more important to pour love from your being into the space. I have a feeling that there will be resistance."

"So we are simply supposed to sit down and vibrate with positivity?" Rudolf asked. "This feels too easy."

Rory shook his head. "Don't discount how difficult it will be when facing evil. It is harder to maintain love when facing hatred than it is for the latter to conform to its adversary, so keep that in mind."

Unconcerned about the bones and glass under him, Rudolf took a seat, peacefully assuming the lotus position. "Okay, I won't be corrupted by the forces battling the House."

Rory nodded, believing that if anyone could maintain love in the face of pure evil, it would be the fae before him. Some people were just inherently good.

# CHAPTER FIFTY-ONE

"She's close," Trudy said in a hushed voice.

Liv knew she was referring to her sister, believing that the seer could sense Hester, the healer.

"On this level?" Stefan asked when they came to the next landing.

"Yes," Trudy answered, her chin down as she peered into the dark. Specters flew back and forth in the hallway ahead. Since the evil spirits were taking possession of the council members, the team decided that unless they were close enough to tell that it wasn't one of the Royals, it was better not to shoot.

"We will leave you here, then," Liv said, gazing up at the top story of the House, where she was certain she'd find Clark and Raina.

Trudy simply nodded as Liv and Stefan continued to ascend.

"Oh, and Warrior Beaufont?" Trudy said when they were halfway up.

Liv turned. "Please don't tell me how to avoid my death."

Trudy actually smiled. "I think we all know that the secret to life isn't in how we die. It's in how we live. When the time comes, do not hesitate to save us all, because you're the only one who can. That's always been the case."

"But it's Papa who…"

The knowledge on Trudy's face cut off Liv's words. "It's always been you, Liv. All prophecies from the beginning have been consistent in that regard."

"So we survive? I save…the people and stuff?" Liv asked, not sure how to put it.

Trudy tilted her head, her smile disappearing. "No. There is no certainty in this future, but if we *are* saved, it will be because of something you do. Good luck, my friend."

Liv nodded as she turned back to the stairs.

"No pressure, then," Stefan remarked.

"No, there really isn't," Liv said dismissively, wishing she had her cape as the cold winds swept through the House. She'd left it over the head of Medusa, but only after taking Papa Creola's package. "I can't do any of this without you all, and you know that. I couldn't have freed Papa Creola or fought Medusa if not for everyone's help."

"I know no one else who would have faced that monster blindfolded, depending on others to help her through it," Stefan stated as they came to the highest story.

"We don't do anything alone in this lifetime, Stefan, but it's taken me a long time to realize that."

"Better late than never," he said, a smile in his voice as they stepped into the hallway.

Liv felt Bellator tug her to the right, in the direction of the library. Of course, her brother would seek refuge there. She hoped that was where he had gone to escape, rather than be a prisoner.

She turned as Stefan faced her. "I think Raina is down there." He pointed to the left.

"Okay, then I leave you to get your sister."

The demon hunter reached out, grabbing her by the wrist and pulling her into him, so there was practically no space between them. He glided his fingers along her jaw, looking deep into her eyes. "I just need you to know that no matter what happens, I—"

"Don't," she interrupted, feeling the goodbye on his lips.

"Don't tell you I love you?" he dared to ask, a wolfish grin on his face. "Are you going to deprive me of maybe the last chance I'll get to tell you that I've loved you since you stumbled through the Door of Reflection, tripping and screaming, changing the stuffy feel of the Chamber forever?"

Liv pinched her lips together, letting out a low growl at the man before her.

Stefan, unaffected by her act of intimidation, continued, "Are you not going to allow me to tell you that if I had any choice about loving, then it was over the moment you made your first smart-ass remark to Adler Sinclair?"

She tried to plaster a frustrated expression on her face, but this man always melted her tough exterior. Liv smiled back at him despite herself.

Stefan went on, "And please don't deprive me of telling you that I was absolutely devoted to you before you saved me from a demon's bite. The thought of abandoning me never even occurring to you. It's not hard to love you, Liv. The only thing that has ever confounded me about you is how you do everything with a grace and mystery that is magic unlike any I've ever witnessed."

"Stefan," Liv said, gripping his hands tighter.

He rolled his neck. "I know. We have people to save and a war to win. I know the timing of this is—"

"No," Liv said, cutting him off, "what you don't get is that I didn't have any choice but to save you. Since you showed up in the corridor covered in sheep's blood, pretending to hunt down innocent magicians, and later dressed as F. Scott Fitzgerald at the All Hallows Eve party, I've been unable to resist you. There was no reality where I was going to allow you to die from a demon's bite or anything else, so whatever you face down that corridor, don't die."

He laughed, pressing her into him tighter. "Of course, you had to outdo me and my speech. I just can't compete with you."

Liv pressed her face into his shoulder, breathing him in. "And the good thing is, you never have to compete with me because you're my equal. You always have been."

Those last four words unleashed a spell the two magicians were unaware of. One that within seconds would reveal to them how intertwined they'd always been.

Stefan's fingers found Liv's chin resting against his chest and gently brought it up so she was staring into his eyes. The kiss that followed wasn't like any they'd shared before. It didn't speak of their caged desires and unfulfilled wishes.

Instead, it was a kiss that spanned centuries, bringing

up memories that lived deep within Liv's bones. Deep within Stefan's. It was the spell Liv's words had unleashed, showing them how eternal their love for one another was.

Liv felt herself in other bodies, as a mortal, as a fae, as many other races in different lives. She saw herself surviving the construction of the pyramids. She saw herself fighting famine and rallying in the streets for women's suffrage. And in all those lifetimes, Liv's soul had loved Stefan's.

There were some who were meant to be, tied together through space and time, no matter the setting.

Liv and Stefan had that timeless love, with no beginning and certainly no end.

# CHAPTER FIFTY-TWO

The library, Liv's favorite place in the House, was bordering on complete destruction. The roof had been pulled off and pages flew around, whipping her in the face as she ran through the large space.

It felt like at any moment, a tornado was about to drop into the expansive floor of the library and sweep Liv away. She barreled through the chaos, ducking shelving that had come loose and was flying around.

Ahead, a specter roared like a train, charging in her direction. Liv held Bellator in front of her, not flinching as the monster crossed the space, howling. When it was almost on her, she swung her sword like a bat, slicing through the beast.

It exploded into sparks, sending brightness over the otherwise dark library.

Liv caught an image just above her. She squinted, trying to see what was blowing in the vortex overhead. Her heart sank when she saw Clark suspended between two specters, appearing to be pulled in half.

He was unconscious, and his head lolled to the side as his pressed shirt flapped in the wind. The evil monsters were bits of shadows, yanking and pulling at her brother like in a game of tug-of-war. It would only be a matter of seconds before they tore him in two.

With her feet shoulder-width apart, Liv held both hands up to the dark sky. Uttering a silent prayer, she unleashed two fireballs. At first, she thought they'd hit Clark, knocking him out of the House entirely, but they swerved several times, pushed off course by the wind. However, Liv wasn't done playing hardball with the evil that had infected her home. She redirected the fireballs, using her magic and as much of her focus as it took until they found the right targets.

The fireballs hit the specters in the center of their shadowy beings and exploded, blowing them into sparks like fireworks as Clark was dropped back down to the floor. Liv conjured a mattress under him, which broke his fall. He hit it, covered in sweat and incoherent.

"Clark?" Liv shook his shoulders, feeling for his breath in his chest. It was slow and low, but it was there. "Clark," she cried again.

Her brother's eyes fluttered, but he appeared locked in sleep, the same as the Mortal Seven. That wasn't going to do. There was no way she would allow that.

Conjuring a bucket of water, Liv poured it on his head like she used to when they were young. He bolted upright, sputtering as he shook his head, looking around and trying to figure out what had happened. When he had finally calmed, Liv smiled at him as she waited for him to realize where they were.

His chest rose and fell with deep breaths.

"Welcome back," she said.

Clark looked at the starry sky overhead and the chaos that still surrounded them. "Liv…"

"Yeah, the House has gone to shit," she stated matter-of-factly.

"But you're here," he said, and there was hope in his voice.

Liv laid her hand on the top of his. "I'd never leave you. And this fight isn't over."

She stood, walking backward. "I have to go, though. Can you…I don't know, put a roof back on this place? Reshelf some books. It's a real mess."

Still disoriented, he looked up as if realizing where he was finally. "Oh, yeah. That's going to take some work, but I'll see what I can do. Where are you going?"

"I have a feeling someone is going to need my help at the eleventh hour," she stated.

Clark nodded. "Be careful, Liv. *Familia est Sempiternum.*" He kissed two fingers and held them up to his little sister.

As she backed for the exit, Liv kissed her first two fingers and raised them. *"Familia est Sempiternum."*

# CHAPTER FIFTY-THREE

L iv took the stairs three at a time, sending fireballs at
specters that sped in her direction. She was hoping
to catch sight of Stefan or one of the other Warriors, but
they were obviously fighting their own battles, doing what
they did best.

She didn't stop when she reached the bottom floor of
the House. Instead, she threw the large door out of the way
and sprinted into the space where the Black Void had been.
She'd hoped to find Plato there, doing whatever Papa
Creola had assigned to him, but he wasn't there, and there
was no sign of the spiraling darkness.

To Liv's surprise, what she found was the most amusing
sight she'd seen in…well, maybe all her life.

Sitting cross-legged in the long corridor of the House
were Rudolf and Rory. Gone were the black vines and
splatters of blood. The walls weren't repaired, but the
destruction appeared to have been halted. Liv even thought
she saw a bit of the gold that used to grace the walls shimmering, trying to break free from under the dark exterior.

The fae and the giant were sitting across from one another, picking dandelions from a patch of grass beside them.

"You know what I like best about you?" Rudolf asked Rory, handing him a flower.

The giant took it. "What?"

"You have a nice smile."

Rory actually blushed, making Liv wonder if the House was now causing her to hallucinate.

"You know what I like about you?" Rory asked the fae.

Liv coughed, realizing they must be drunk on something since they hadn't even noticed her there.

Unhurriedly, they glanced up, a dreamy quality in their eyes. "Well, there she is. The most beautiful Warrior." Rudolf batted his eyes at her.

"Are you guys drunk?" Liv asked.

Rory shook his head. "We're killing the negativity infecting this part of the House."

"With?" Liv asked.

"Love," Rudolf answered. He then dared to shoo her away. "Now you go fight, because your anxious nature is making it hard to concentrate on unicorns and giggling babies."

"I like thinking about skipping rocks and autumn days," Rory said, his tone full of giddiness.

Rudolf fired a finger at him. "Good one, old pal."

Backing away, Liv nodded. "Okay. Good work, fellas."

It did appear that the giant and fae were doing their job, although they were using unorthodox means. She expected nothing less from those two.

After Liv sped out of the corridor, she came to a halt,

breathless at the sight before her. Plato's form was dim but growing brighter by the second.

Liv took a careful step forward. "Plato, are you okay?"

The lynx nodded. "I'm fine. A few lives down, but I did what Papa Creola asked."

"A few?" she asked, her heart skipping.

"It's fine, Liv," he stated. "I did what I had to do to close the Black Void."

She glanced at the wall beside them. It did appear solid for the first time she could remember. Placing her hand against the wall, she felt a soft heartbeat.

*Thump. Thump.*

Liv pulled her hand back like she'd been shocked. "You closed it? Is that safe?"

"It was supposed to be a haven for those seeking refuge from persecution, but it turned into a place for Talon to hibernate," Plato explained. "The only way to cut off the negative thoughts he'd spun inside the House was to cut *it* off."

"Won't the House need a mind?" Liv asked.

He shook his head. "Not if the people who run it think for themselves and make it so there's not a need for a safe haven."

"Oh." Liv looked at the solid wall and then Plato. "It's hard to believe Talon came about from a place meant for good. That he came out the way he did. That any of this happened the way it did."

Plato nodded. "As a great man who shares my name once said, 'This and no other is the root from which a tyrant springs; when he first appears he is a protector.'"

Liv nodded, realizing that Talon had lasted as long as he

SARAH NOFFKE & MICHAEL ANDERLE

had because he had deceived the founders, the Mortal Seven, and his ancestors into believing just that. But his days were done. At least, she hoped they were.

Taking a step toward the Door of Reflection, she chanced a glance at Plato. "Are you coming with me?"

He smiled. "I think we both know I'll always be by your side."

CHAPTER FIFTY-FOUR

For the first time ever, there were no visions from the Door of Reflection. Liv realized that was because she was stepping into what was by far her worst nightmare, but she walked through willingly.

The Chamber of the Tree appeared similar to the House, with howling winds and bleeding walls. All the Mortal Seven were slumped over, their chimeras in pet form beside them. Liv's eyes weren't able to find John before her attention was stolen by the fight ensuing in the middle of the room.

Talon in his long white robes and matching hair hovered in front of the tree, his spotlight eyes directed at Papa Creola.

The father of time darted to the side as a beam of green light shot in his direction.

"I'm too powerful to be stopped," Talon growled. "I've taken the power of the founders and the House."

Papa Creola's chin swiveled to the side, his eyes barely catching Liv in his peripheral vision. "What you have never understood is that real power doesn't come from the major sources."

Talon laughed, sending a barreling wind at Papa Creola and knocking him to the side.

Liv wanted to rush to him as he careened into the wall, but she knew something very important was in play. She simply watched.

"When you are gone, I'll finally rise, ruling as I was always intended to do," Talon spat, sending a charge of electricity at the gnome. It caught the bottom of his shoe, and he toppled backward and landed on his head.

Liv didn't expect to see Papa Creola battling in such an ungraceful manner. It baffled her. However, she noticed that on the bench, the Mortal Seven's chimeras were stirring.

Talon laughed, enjoying the damage he'd done to Papa Creola as the gnome clambered to his feet, shaking his head. At his side, his fingers twitched, reminding Liv of silent spells she'd done when she didn't want her enemies to know what she was doing.

"If you rule, Talon," Papa Creola stated, sounding breathless, "there will be nothing left."

The man who called himself a god hovered over the father of time. "If I'm the last one left, I've won. As long as there are no more mortals remaining, I'll be the victor."

He swept his hand to the side, and it threw Papa Creola against the wall with an awful cracking sound.

Talon's eyes slid to Liv, who was standing stock-still. "Have you come to watch him die?"

Liv didn't say a word, although she wanted to rush over and help up the crumpled gnome laying on the floor.

"When I'm done, I'll deal with you, Olivia Beaufont," Talon stated, zooming over to where Papa Creola was lying.

Again she saw Pickles' ear twitch. Harry's tail flickered next to Ireland, and Freya's wings fluttered next to Cassie.

Liv wasn't sure what was happening, but something told her it was part of Papa Creola's strategy. She could only hope so as Talon took the father of time in his grasp and began choking the life out of him. Liv wanted to rush over and stop him. She started to but heard a loud and clear, *No!* in her mind.

The blood beat in her head as a very distinct message traveled across her thoughts. "We can knock down our enemies with a sweep of our hand, but the better way, the more sustainable way, is to build forces that will knock our enemies down and keep them there. That's what a real leader does. They build other leaders up because that's what the world will always need—more to champion the fight."

Liv listened to the message repeat, knowing who the voice belonged to. Papa Creola.

She watched as the small man's body was broken by attacks from Talon. He didn't stop as blood seeped from Papa Creola's nostrils. He didn't back down when the father of time didn't fight back. Talon never questioned why his opponent wasn't fighting back, and therefore he never noticed as every single chimera on the bench transformed into its purest form behind him.

Standing regally at Talon Sinclair's back were seven full-sized chimeras, their lion heads held high, their serpent tails swishing, and their goat eyes narrowed with vengeance.

Talon reached forward, scooping up the nearly limp body of Papa Creola and holding it high. Liv could hardly watch, although she knew looking away wasn't an option.

"And now your reign is done, Father Time!" Talon yelled, his voice shaking the Chamber of the Tree. "It's my turn!"

The betrayer of the House of Fourteen, the one who killed Liv's parents and siblings, broke the fragile body he held in his hands, severing a life that was the seedling of this planet. It had been Papa Creola and Mother Earth who had started this world on its strange and beautiful voyage, and now…he was gone.

But those he had fueled with his strength rose on their hind legs, their teeth bared, ready to pounce.

Talon threw the gnome's body across the chamber, showing no respect for the man who had lived for all of time. Then he turned his sunbeam eyes on Liv, a brutal grimace on his face. "Are you ready to meet the same end as your master? As your family, Olivia Beaufont?"

"Sure," Liv said casually. "But two things, real quick. Firstly, my name is Liv." Like before, when she had launched the two fireballs into the sky to save Clark, Liv held her arms wide, sending out a command from the bottom of her soul. "And secondly, rise up, chimeras, protectors of the Mortal Seven, and attack the one who has broken the magical world. The one who thinks of himself as a god, but forever will be condemned to the pits of hell where he belongs."

As if starting a drag race, Liv brought both her arms down, her head bowed, and then shot straight back up.

Talon was more than confused, but his reality quickly dawned on him as the chorus of growls echoed at his back. The magician hovered, then descended several inches as the implications sank in. He turned, his sunbeam eyes dimming slightly. The man backed up. Dropped to the ground. Tried to send attacks, but he'd used all his strength taking down Papa Creola. He was no match for one chimera, and he was helpless against seven of them.

In unison, the chimeras launched off the bench the council shared, their mouths wide. Each attacked a different part of Talon, ripping and pulling him apart bit by bit, making him utter howls unlike any Liv had ever heard. They brought the mass of white skin, robes, and hair to the floor of the chamber, yanking him into pieces like wild animals on the hunt, desperately wanting their portion of the kill.

Liv watched, unable to pull her eyes from the demise of the worst evil the world had ever known. She needed to know that Talon Sinclair was gone. She needed to know that it had worked. That was why she didn't look away until every part of him had disappeared through the worst means ever—being eaten alive by enemies he had underestimated.

## CHAPTER FIFTY-FIVE

When Talon Sinclair was only bones, Liv expected the Mortal Seven to awaken. They didn't.

The chimeras circled the chamber, giving her confused expressions like they expected her to rouse their masters. Liv searched the chamber, her eyes finding Papa Creola's limp body.

She began to tremble and then realized it wasn't just her. It was the ground under her feet. The dome over her. Everything around Liv was shaking.

She spun, searching the dome as the lights representing magicians flickered and dimmed. The tree did the same.

Liv didn't understand. "We defeated Talon. Now what?"

"The world can't live without *him*," Plato stated at her side, real remorse in his voice.

Liv blinked at him, not knowing who he was referring to at first. Her eyes skipped to the broken body of the gnome. "You don't mean…"

Plato didn't answer, but she knew what his expression meant.

"But…" She realized at once that any excuse she had didn't matter. Her end was an acceptable reality if it meant the continuation of the world she loved.

Liv withdrew the sealed package Papa Creola had left her. With shaking fingers, she opened it, her tears falling so hard and fast they soaked the paper. Like vinegar on baking soda, her tears fizzed and bubbled when they spattered the smooth black stone about the size of a dime that was inside the wrapping. It was like Papa Creola himself: unassuming, small, and perfect.

With her eyes still overflowing with tears, Liv looked at Plato questioningly.

"You know what to do," Plato stated. "If you don't, I can't tell you, dear Liv. This only works if it comes from you."

She hated riddles. She hated that the people around her knew the answers but kept them to themselves.

Liv Beaufont also loved everything about this world. It was worth preserving, even if she couldn't be a part of it. Her pulse beat in her fingers that held the stone and it was the pulse of the universe, which only had minutes before it would crumble, unable to last long without its source.

Without a second of hesitation, Liv placed both her hands around the stone, pressing her palms together tightly. Her shirt was soaked by her tears, but that didn't deter her from what she did next.

Liv sent all her magic into the stone that carried the essence of Papa Creola, feeding the last living part of the father of time. Nurturing him, bringing him to life for what wouldn't be the last time, but would certainly be the last for Liv.

The stone exploded in Liv's hands, knocking her back into the wall of the chamber. Her skull cracked and her spine broke from the force, but she didn't let go of her hold on this world. Nor did she cry out as her last few breaths, devoid of magic, whistled from her nostrils.

Instead, she watched as the most beautiful sight materialized in front of her. It was the Big Bang. It was the beginning of time. It was the birth of something new.

The stone, carrying the essence of Papa Creola and fueled by her magic, rose into the air, stardust radiating off it, before it shined so bright that it burned Liv's eyes too badly to watch.

Whatever happened next, Liv didn't see, because she was swept away from that world to one she'd only seen in dreams.

# CHAPTER FIFTY-SIX

G uinevere Beaufont lay beside her daughter for as long as she could. Theodore kissed Olivia Beaufont's head, his lips never really touching her. The pair watched over their daughter, knowing that she wasn't meant for their world, or not for at least a hundred years.

The greatest Warrior the House of Fourteen had ever known hadn't died, and yet she wasn't quite alive.

She was broken, sure. She was stuck, yes. But that was nothing that couldn't be repaired if one knew the right people—or rather, worked for him.

The ghosts watched over their daughter, as they had done every day since their deaths, waiting for the moment the prophecy had spoken of but no one had told Olivia about.

---

Liv lay in the center of the Chamber of the Tree, the

Mortal Seven and Councilors all looking down at her, their chimeras beside them. Behind her, standing in their spots, were the remaining Warriors, without Akio and Maria, casualties of what would later be called the Last War.

Jude and Diabolos stood on either side of the bench, their faces impassive. And beside Liv, was an elf with clear blue eyes, a ponytail, and a crooked chin. He wore running shorts, no shirt, and a pair of earbuds as he hummed, running his hands over Liv's body.

Rudolf kept knocking Rory in the side, whispering to him from the corner of his mouth. The giant simply swatted at the fae like he was a pesky fly.

"Be quiet," he encouraged.

"But is she going to wake up?"

"Yes, but what she'll be is still unclear," Rory explained. "She had to burn out her magic to bring Papa Creola back."

Rudolf shook his head. "If he regenerated, why did he come back as an old hippie marathoner?"

Rory rolled his eyes, his usual response to one of Rudolf's statements. "He has his reasons."

The giant lifted his gaze to spy Clark staring down at his sister as Papa Creola repaired her body. He always wanted to take away people's pain, secretly being an empath. However, never before had he wanted to erase so many people's pain, including his own. Feeling Clark's despair and Stefan's utter sadness was too much. The chamber was filled with more grief than Rory could handle.

That was why he finally broke, covering his face and crying, not knowing if the tears would ever stop. He didn't even object when Rudolf wrapped his arms around his waist and pulled him in tightly.

"It's okay, big guy," Rudolf said, patting his lower back, which was the highest place he could touch.

## CHAPTER FIFTY-SEVEN

L iv knew she wasn't dead, but she wasn't anywhere close to how she'd been. Before she even opened her eyes, she tried to pinpoint what was different.

She tilted her chin from side to side. Her broken skull had been fixed.

Mutters filled the chamber. "She's stirring." "She's moving." "Look."

Liv wiggled her back, feeling the chamber floor under her body.

*My spine isn't broken,* she realized.

That much was clear with her eyes shut, but there was still something that wasn't right. Or maybe it just wasn't normal.

A strange prickling sensation touched Liv's forehead, making her eyes spring open as she shot into a sitting position.

The chamber, fuller than she'd ever seen it, erupted in chatter. Liv couldn't pay them any attention as she coughed, feeling like her lungs were liquid and going to come right out her mouth.

"There you go," a man said, clapping her on the back. "The first breath is always the hardest to take."

"First…" Liv sputtered on a cough, holding her chest, "breath?"

The man was an elf; she recognized that at once, seeing his pointy ears. What she couldn't understand was why he was shirtless and looked like he was about to take a run in his tight-laced sneakers and sweat shorts.

"Well, your first second breath of this life," the man said, holding out his bony hands to her. "Now, like a fawn, it's better if you try standing and walking as quickly after birth as possible."

"Birth?" Liv asked, looking around and recognizing the faces of the Councilors, the Mortal Seven, the Warriors, and her friends. Plato stood on her right, a pirate smile on the lynx's mouth, although she wasn't sure why.

"The last thing I remember is…" Liv's eyes widened. "I died."

The man shook his head. "Not quite. You burned out your magic to bring me back."

Liv tilted her head to the side with confusion, then her eyes grew wide. "Papa Creola?"

He must have been the same person because the elf simply nodded. "Yes, you gave me what I needed to regenerate."

Liv didn't care that he'd hate her for it, she threw her arms around his shoulders, realizing how thin he was. He needed a steak and some couch time.

Humoring her, he simply patted Liv on the back. "Now, up. We need to stand. Walk."

Liv did as she was told, trying to remember the battle, Talon, and the chimeras. "I burned out my magic?" she asked, finding that her legs were wobbly under her.

"Yes," he said matter-of-factly. "And you sustained many injuries that should have killed you."

Still confused, Liv kept hold of the elf's hand as he led her forward. She felt so strange, seemingly taking her first steps in front of the mostly silent audience. It felt like they should all be celebrating instead of watching her. They should be repairing the House or doing anything but standing there, putting way too much attention on her.

After she took several steps, she turned around, running her gaze over the curious faces. "Why are they all staring at me?"

Papa Creola, finally her height, leaned in and whispered in her ear, "You burned out your magic to bring me back."

And only on the second time saying that did it compute for Liv.

It felt like she died again. Liv wouldn't be a Warrior. She wouldn't be a magician. She'd be…herself.

Reluctantly, but trying to find a place of acceptance, Liv nodded. "Okay." She looked around, grateful to see Stefan staring at her, his beautiful charisma bouncing in his eyes. Beside him was Trudy, her face battered but very much alive. She brought her attention back to Papa Creola. "Talon is gone?"

He nodded.

"And the House?"

"It will survive," he answered.

"But it was broken so badly," she stated.

"The House is an organic, living creature," he explained. "All they need to grow or regrow is love and nourishment. Simply give it that, and it will come back in time."

Liv gulped, looking around and finding John staring down at her. And Raina, and so many other kind faces. "Well, I'm not dead. I'm not what I used to be, but as long as this world has a chance at peace, I'm fine."

She was surprised when Papa Creola, not a being known for affection, took her hand in both of his. He lowered his head, his pointy ears directed at her like antlers. "And that is exactly what every person in this world can choose when they meet a challenge. They can look at the good, or they regret the loss." In Papa Creola's hand, Liv's glowed. It didn't hurt, but she was also sure the feeling that radiated through her arm and down her spine wasn't normal.

When he released her, Liv snapped straight. "What did you do?"

"I made you something different," Papa Creola answered, a hint of mischief in his usually neutral voice. "I made you what you already were. You, Liv Beaufont, are the stuff of legends, and now you'll live as long as one."

"What?" she asked as the chamber of people gasped.

"I doubled your lifespan," Papa Creola said with a wink. "That way, you'll live as long as your soulmate."

Liv's face burned hotly, feeling Stefan's eyes on her. "Oh, my gosh. But why?"

"Because you gave up your life for others when any other option would have been what most would have chosen," he answered.

Liv couldn't understand, but she didn't argue with the man before her. She simply rubbed her fingers together, feeling some sort of electricity in them. With a furrowed brow, she lifted her hands, staring at them. "Papa, if I burned up all my magic then why…"

"Why does it feel stronger than ever?" he asked, obviously hiding a smile. "Well, when you're the boss of this world, you get to do what you damn well please, and I can't have my best agent powerless."

"Only agent!" Rudolf corrected. "And can I get a job?"

Papa Creola shook his head at the fae. "Not a chance, King."

"You gave me back my magic?" Liv asked, staring in disbelief at the man before her.

He shook his head. "Oh, no. *You* earned your magic back. *You* earned a long life. No one is ever given anything in this lifetime that they didn't somehow earn. Believe me, I have the experience to know that firsthand."

---

And so the prophecy had come true. The rebellious sister had become the stuff of legends. Not because she wanted power. Not because she wanted fame. But because she cared about justice and people and the love that made the world go around.

Guinevere and Theodore Beaufont had known that their daughter would go on to do amazing things, but not until they watched her take her second first breath did they know that she'd in fact saved the world, ensuring the sun would rise yet again and for many years to come.

# CHAPTER FIFTY-EIGHT

Getting reborn was weird. Liv reminded herself that she hadn't really died as she tried to reorganize her walk-in pantry in her industrial-sized kitchen.

"I think I need to go back to the way things were before," she said to Plato, hoofing it six yards to put the Himalayan salt with the other sixteen types of salt in the pantry.

"You don't like being a consumer?" he asked from his perch on the top shelf.

She shook her head. "I liked my small studio apartment that I could clean and have a manageable rack full of spices. More just brings complications."

"Do you really want to go back to living in that closet?" Plato asked.

Liv thought for a moment. "No, but a happy medium would be nice. Nothing too small but nothing unmanageable."

"It's thinking like that which made Papa Creola give you your magic back and extend your life," Plato said.

"Like what?"

"You never take more than you need and always give more than you have," he stated.

Liv picked up a can of melted cheese, ideas for snack options springing into her head. "Yeah, I'm still really confused about the whole thing. I felt like I died."

"But you didn't."

"I felt like I'd lost everything."

"When, in fact, you'd gained everything."

"I guess it will just take a while to process, which is why I'm glad to have this time alone," she stated, looking up at the lynx and finding him gone.

Liv blew out a breath, annoyed at Plato, but also not at all.

"I might have picked an inopportune time to visit you based on your last statement," a man said in a deep voice with an accent from behind Liv.

She tensed, not just because Bellator was on the living room table or she was drowsy from sleeping all day, but also because she was hardly dressed in pajama shorts and a tank top.

Tentatively, she turned to find a man she'd characterize as a Scottish warrior standing in the doorway of her pantry.

"Ummm. If you're here to deliver the pizza I ordered, I haven't ordered it yet," she stated, noticing that the man's hands were on his thick waist. He was wearing armor, and fur pelts covered his shoulders. His dark beard and mustache were lush, and his head was shaved on the sides, the top slicked back. He wore many rings on his fingers, which he clanged with slight irritation against the hilt of his sheathed sword. And to make him all the more interesting, he wore a blue and green kilt, which Liv would have never partnered with black leather hiking boots and high socks. But no one was calling her for fashion advice, so what did she know?

The man shook his head. "I'm not here to deliver a pizza."

*No shit,* Liv thought, trying to figure out the man's age. He didn't appear to be more than forty, yet she got the impression he'd seen more centuries than Rudolf, which was impressive.

"Who are you?" Liv asked.

He took a step back, unblocking her way out of the pantry. "My name is Hiker. I'm the leader of the Dragon Elite."

Liv had started forward carrying her can of cheese but halted. "Hiker. That's a cool name. Were your parents hippies?"

He narrowed his eyes at her. "No. Vikings, actually."

Pretending to be looking for a pan in her large kitchen, Liv simply nodded. "Cool. I'm French. Why did you break and enter my place, Hiker?"

The large man watched her look into different cabinets, shutting them almost at once. "I thought you might be able to help me with something."

Liv stood. "Sure, sure," she said, her nervousness bounding out of her chest. This man was here for Sophia, but he couldn't have her. Not yet. "Thing is, I'm on vacation for, like, three or four days. I just saved the world from destruction, so I took off a day or two. Maybe you can ring me back at that time?"

This guy appreciated her jokes as much as Papa Creola, based on his stony expression. "This won't take much of your time."

Liv pretended to yawn. "Cool. But real quickly, how'd you get in here?" she asked. "I have wards that prevent intruders."

"I think we both know those don't apply to me," Hiker stated.

*Lovely*, Liv thought, pulling a bowl out of a cabinet and emptying the can of cheese into it. "Well, since I'm definitely not intimidated by having an armed man standing in my kitchen while I heat up queso, why don't you tell me why you're here? I'm planning on watching Netflix all night and need to start soon to make that happen."

He grimaced at her. "What's Netflix?"

Liv held in her reaction. Sophia was going to fit in with this guy like an iPhone among typewriters. "It's nothing. Anywho, what's the reason you are making me feel uncomfortable in my home again? Oh, that's right, you have yet to tell me why you came in here when I wasn't wearing a bra. But don't worry, I'm the forgiving type."

Hiker's mustache fluttered as he let out a long breath. "The Elite have ways of telling when new dragon riders have been born, come of age, or magnetized to an egg. We have reason to believe all three of those things have happened, and my indications say that they've happened close to you, Warrior Beaufont. Do you know what I'm talking about?"

Liv tapped her finger on her lips, pretending to think.

"Dragon rider? Egg? Extra side of guacamole? No, I have no idea what you're talking about."

He narrowed his eyes at her. "I believe I didn't say anything about guacamole. What is that, anyway?"

Liv gauged the man before her. "The Elite get out, right?"

He simply shifted his eyes back and forth like her question didn't deserve an answer.

"Okay, fine, Mr. Hiker. I don't know what you're referring to. I've been defeating an evil magician who was pretty close to ending the world as we know it." Liv stuck her hands on her hips. "Actually, where were the Elite when the world was spinning into a black hole? Why weren't you all helping?"

Annoyance skipped to his eyes. "We were well aware of how things fell apart when Talon Sinclair tried to control the House."

"So, you've got a one-for-all mentality, then?" Liv dared to ask.

"We abandoned the House when we realized the magicians needed to figure things out on their own. Solve things for their own. Your problems shouldn't be ours."

Liv could feel Hiker's magic, which was more powerful than hers, although she'd never admit that to the man. "How is it that you, a magician, could abandon your own?"

His rings clanged against the hilt of his sword. "I'm a dragon rider."

"Right, and this world ending and Father Time dying is not going to affect you. Oh, wait, it totally would," she refuted.

"Look, Warrior Beaufont, the Elite weren't interested in

voting on matters related to the House when things were corrupt. If that has changed, then we will consider it again. But the matters we deal with are much bigger than your scope."

"Like?" Liv asked.

He simply stared at her.

"Okay, so we still have some trust to build," Liv said, throwing up her hands. "Maybe we should do a ropes course together or something."

"So you're not aware of a dragon rider in your midst?" Hiker asked.

Liv shook her head. "No, I-I-I've been busy. But if I do hear of a dragon rider, how should I contact you?"

"I'll be in contact with *you*," Hiker stated. "If you so much sense that a dragon rider is in your community, I want to hear about him. This is of supreme importance. I must be the first to know about him."

Liv nodded. "Absolutely. I'll let you know if I hear anything about *him*. Now will you be staying for nachos? I was planning on watching reruns of *Parks and Rec*. You interested? I love Amy Poehler."

The dragon rider simply shook his head at her like she was an alien offering to make him eggs on her spaceship.

Hiker took a step closer to Liv, the many talismans and weapons on his belt rattling. "Just so you know, Warrior Beaufont, we start off as friends, but I caution you, don't make an enemy of me. None of mine survive."

Liv force a smile to her face. "Sure. Totally. And no enemies here. Just an offer to curl up on the couch and watch shows with melted cheese."

Hiker simply shook his head at her before disappearing.

Liv rolled her eyes. "People who can teleport are so boring."

Plato materialized beside her, flicking his tail. "I agree."

# CHAPTER FIFTY-NINE

Bermuda thought the music from the stage was too loud, but Rory had promised her that he and Maddie had put adequate silencing charms around his property. For that one night, the giant's yard had been expanded to fit everyone Liv invited to the celebration.

Sophia's dragon egg had been moved to the center island, where most wouldn't venture due to the lava and many other wards. Still, Liv trusted everyone at this party. It was the event of the century. The one to celebrate the new House of Fourteen.

"Are you sure that music isn't too loud?" Bermuda asked, covering her ears as Rooster's band Moldy Oranges began to play another song.

Liv nodded her head to the music. "It's better loud."

The giantess shook her head. "I think I'm overdue for an excursion."

"Where will your travels take you this time?" Liv asked, yelling to be heard over the music.

The giantess simply darted her eyes around the yard.

"You know," Liv imparted, "you are about as forthcoming as that dragon rider who invaded my apartment."

"About that," Bermuda stated.

"Yes?" Liv asked, her hands on her hips.

Bermuda straightened the large hat on her curly head. "Well, based on what you told me, you handled it well."

"So, you said the Dragon Elite were pretty much gone." Liv watched as Rooster rocked out with his guitar, ironically noticing how much heart he put into his performance. It made her very happy.

"Well, that was what we thought," Bermuda stated. "But they are obviously somewhere. Only Sophia will know soon. They have strict laws that keep dragon riders from telling anyone about their society, which is why I don't say anything about it in the books."

"Yes, Hiker wasn't a real open sort of guy, although I think the next time I might be able to get him to put up his boots and watch a show with me," Liv said, then added, "Although on second thought, I might have him keep his feet down if he's wearing the kilt."

"Liv, I don't know much about the Dragon Elite, but I do know that technology isn't a part of their lives," Bermuda imparted. "Sophia and her egg might not fit in really well with them."

Liv watched from a distance as her sister twirled and danced with her friends in front of the stage as the band rocked out. Her werewolf friend Fane and his daughter Alina took turns twirling Sophia. "I think she'll be just fine. She might even make a difference."

Bermuda watched Sophia shaking her hips next to the stage. "That's exactly what I'm worried about."

Liv turned to face the giantess. "I'm not. Sometimes someone different is exactly what an organization needs."

Bermuda didn't appear so sure, but when her son sidled up next to Liv, she simply nodded. "Do you have my travel itinerary in case you need anything?"

"Yes, mum," Rory answered.

"And if you need help with decisions about House business—"

Liv shook her head, holding up a hand to silence Bermuda. "It's his vote. You raised him right. He'll make the right decisions."

The giantess looked out at the crowd, where Rudolf was currently body-surfing. "You're right. Now, whether the king of the fae makes the right decisions? Well, that's another story."

Rory smiled down at Liv. "I don't know. Rudolf is different, but at the end of the day, he votes on matters with his heart. I have faith in him."

Whatever Rory and Rudolf had been through in Medusa's temple or the House in the final battle had bonded them more than ever. They had become quite close, and it was great for both of them.

"Rory, this is my favorite of the Moldy Oranges songs," Maddie exclaimed, rushing forward and pulling the giant away. He waved as he was dragged to the front of the stage to dance next to many of the people Liv had gotten to know through strange circumstances over that year. Mortimer was there with Pricilla and Ticker, and so was Renswick Shoshawnawalla. And then, of course, all of the Mortal Seven and the Councilors and Warriors had come.

"So it's final, then?" Bermuda asked. "The House of Fourteen will ask for votes from each race on major laws?"

"Yes," Liv chirped. "And your son is the first giant to advise the House, and Rudolf the first fae. And the king of the elves, Dakota, will be chipping in his vote. We've also got a gnome by the name of Gillian who will represent them. It's progress."

"It's more than has happened in a century," Bermuda stated, her mouth twitching. "And to think, it's all because of... Well, you know."

Liv nodded, not needing the giantess to say anything further as they watched the dancers at the front of the stage.

Finally, Bermuda sighed. "Well, I should be off."

Liv's mouth popped open. "Don't you want to say goodbye to Rory?"

Bermuda looked longingly at her son, who was swing-dancing with Maddie, a wide grin on his face. "No, I don't think so. Not this time." She turned to Liv. "But I do want to say something to you."

Liv straightened, which really made her look silly in front of the giant. "Yes?"

"Warrior Beaufont, you know that you're loved," Bermuda began. "Papa Creola let the magical world know that when he granted you such gifts, but I want you to know that I hope you get the other things you want in your life. I know none that deserve them as much as you do."

Liv opened her mouth to say something, but she didn't know how to respond.

Bermuda pointed through the crowd at the demon hunter, who seemed to be waiting for the giantess to wave him over. He was standing next to Emilio, who had his arm around a female fae. "Well, I'll be off. Until I see you again, take care."

Liv felt distracted as she looked between Bermuda's retreating back and Stefan, who was approaching with the fae and Emilio beside him. She tilted her head to the side. "What's going on, Ludwig?"

He grabbed her hand on one side and her hip on the other, swaying her to the beat of the music. "Nothing. Em and I just thought we'd tell you that the council passed a measure that allows interracial dating among Royals."

Liv yelped, looking over Stefan's shoulder. "That's fantastic! Congrats, Em!"

The fellow warrior pumped his fist as he danced with the gorgeous fae in his arms. "Thank you. And congrats to you."

"Me?" Liv asked, looking sideways at Stefan.

"Oh, about that." He dipped her, and with his face inches from hers, Stefan said, "And they've abolished the laws about Warriors dating. It might complicate things, but I think we're okay with that since we've got a cat, a terrier, a dragonfly, and many other animals making up the council now."

Liv wrapped her hands around his face and pulled him in for a kiss, for the first time, not caring who was watching. And whether the crowd cheered because Rooster's band was awesome or because their kiss sent fireworks into the sky, Liv didn't know. All she cared about was that she could be happy with the people she loved and the job that she cared about.

It wasn't lost on her, as she smashed her lips into

Stefan's, that when she'd started as a Warrior for the House, she was only doing it until Sophia could take over, and now she prayed it would be a life sentence. Few could hope to have a job they enjoyed so much.

For Liv, protecting the world and the ones she loved was all she wanted to do.

It had only taken nearly losing both for her to realize it.

# CHAPTER SIXTY

No one was drinking, but everyone at the party seemed intoxicated. Maybe that was because so many dangers had been removed. The House wasn't repaired, but in time, it would be. The council had diversity, and laws were changing to benefit the people and not the system. Liv couldn't be happier.

"You told me to make an appearance," Papa Creola said, his head low. He was holding a red Solo cup.

"Who is the boss here?" Liv asked with a laugh. She then gawked at the new Subner.

He appeared very similar to Papa Creola, with long, stringy hair and sweatbands around his wrists and forehead.

"Where are you guys headed?" Liv asked. "The Boston Marathon?"

Papa Creola sighed. "Every regeneration of mine is different. I never know what form I will take."

Liv nodded. "Well, I like this one. Is the Fantastical Armory different?"

Subner shook his head. "Oh, no. It's the same. Always."

"It's good to know some things don't change," Liv stated, watching as her brother approached through the crowd, his arm around Sophia.

"I think we better…" Subner said, his voice suddenly searching.

"Check out the bean dip," Papa Creola stated.

Liv wasn't sure why they had rushed off so suddenly or why she felt like darting over and hugging her siblings. It was probably just the rush of all the emotions she felt with all her friends being in the same place at once.

"So," Clark said, smiling and dancing to the music

Liv grimaced at him. "What are you doing?"

"I'm…well, I was *trying* to dance." Clark frowned.

"No, it was good," Sophia said, grabbing her brother's hand and jiving beside him. It was only then that Liv realized how much her little sister had grown. She knew she had. She'd seen it. But her baby sister was out past dark at a late party. It was time Liv admitted to herself that Sophia was moving on to other things.

"Hey, Soph," Liv said, interrupting her siblings' dancing. "Will you and Clark join me over here?"

The pair trotted over, happy to comply. Liv led them to where the dragon's egg was being kept. Liv saw John rushing to join them. "Hey, there you are! I've been looking for you all night."

"I've been here," Liv answered. "Where have you been, John?"

His face sprouted blotches of red suddenly. "Nowhere. I mean, well… Alicia and I might have gotten…"

"News!" Rudolf yelled, rushing over. "I've got news!"

"Yes?" Liv asked.

"Well, Serena and I just found out we're having triplets. So we'll be having Captain, Captain, and Captain." He smirked, his hands on his hips like a proud superhero.

"Wow," Clark said, shaking his head.

"Yeah, that's totally crazy," Sophia added.

Plato materialized next to Liv and looked at the group. "That's really nuts."

John's mouth popped open, his eyes going wide. "Liv, the cat just…"

Liv smiled. "I told you, John. Plato can talk. Pretty cool, huh?"

"It's not triplets-cool," Rudolf stated, his arms over Liv and Sophia's shoulders, the two being the same height.

"No, that definitely takes the cake," Liv said, looking past the fae at her baby sister, who was more beautiful than she'd ever thought possible.

"I'm really happy for you, Rudolf," John said, patting the fae on the back.

Rudolf released Liv and Sophia and put his arm around the first of the Mortal Seven. "Thanks, pal. Can I buy you a drink?"

"Well, I think it's an open bar," John stated.

"Yeah, but the liquor here is pretty cheap, if you ask me," Rudolf whispered too loud. "How about I order in some real drinks?"

"Sounds good, my friend," John said, allowing himself to be led off by the king of the fae.

Liv watched them move away, shocked by how different and wonderful her life had become.

"What is it, Liv?" Clark asked, reading the expression on her face.

She shook her head. "It is just so great. We're all together, and everything feels right. I don't want anything to change, although I know change is inevitable and leads to progress."

Sophia smiled so broadly it brought more happy tears to Liv's face. That seemed to trigger Clark. He wrapped both the girls in a hug, clutching them tightly. "Mom and Dad would be proud. So would Ian and Reese."

Liv nodded, thinking fondly of the family they'd lost who had set the path for them. "No matter what, *Familia est Sempiternum.*"

"No matter what," Clark and Sophia said together.

Liv hugged them tightly before releasing her brother and sister. Wiping the tears from her eyes, she looked at the crowd of people still partying in Rory's backyard. "Well, should we go back and join the party?"

"Yes," Sophia squealed.

"As long as someone teaches me how to dance," Clark stated.

Liv hooked her arms through Sophia's and Clark's. "Don't worry, we've got you covered, brother."

The three strode back in the direction of the stage, but they weren't far when a sound of reckoning cued the next biggest change in their lives.

*Crack.*

The sound reverberated through the yard and over the band so loudly that there was no chance the Dragon Elite hadn't noticed.

A HUGE thank you to everyone for supporting this series. Twelve-freaking-books! I can't believe it. I mean, I can. But man, how freaking awesome. Thank you!

Okay, at some point I want to talk about Michael's Amish ways, but we'll get to that in just a bit. First, I know I need to address Akio's death.

I'm sorry that Akio died in this book. And I'm sorrier than anyone, if you can believe it. If you think I saw Akio Takahashi dying, then you're dead wrong. Sorry, no pun intended there.

Seriously though, I'm all writing that Medusa scene and then I type, "...and the ceiling caved in, crushing Akio." I was like, "BUT wait! What happened to Akio?!" I back-spaced. Tried a different ending for that chapter. Took a walk. Had a drink. Took another walk. Had another drink. Yes, I get that walking won't solve my problems. That's why I drink.

Anyway, it was only after much agony that I realized, there was no other ending. That was the only one. And it hurt. I know you all think I'm an evil author who thirsts for your tears. I, in fact do, and I am an evil author. I'm the first to admit it, but I still have feelings. Okay, just the one actually. I have a feeling. And it really hurt that feeling when Akio died.

I remember going to Taco Bell afterwards...okay, that makes me sound bad. Let's call it Organic-Hippie-Café... with tacos. Anyway, I went there. And I'm crying like a freaking baby in the drive through...I mean, in the line. Since I'd never go anywhere that my car would idle, sending out fumes to the ozone.

So I pull up to the drive through and the teenager is like, "What's wrong Miss?"

I thought, "Besides from the fact that I'm not a Miss and not old enough to be your mother unless....okay, I'm old enough to be your mother, but shut it. And do you have an older brother? Oh, wait...this internal convo went the wrong way."

Anyway, what I actually said was, "Akio died!"

He didn't know who Akio was because he's lame and probably reads assigned books like the dumb Heart of Darkness. Man, I hated that book in freshman English.

My point to this long diatribe is that Akio's death hurt. It hurt like freaking hell. I don't plan these things most of the time. But when they happen, I have to respect them. Akio had to die. But what a selfless way to do so. I freaking love that warrior.

Okay, moving on before I start crying again.

I know you all think that I just do hallucinogens and come up with the random weirdness in the books. Nothing could be further from the truth. I dream it. Without drugs.

So the other day, I wake up after having a dream that Jack Nicholson and I went to Target. I tell Lydia (my daughter) about it and she's like, "What did you buy?" I look at her like, "That's your follow up question?" She didn't want to know what Jack and I talked about or where we went for gelato afterwards?

And that's how random weirdness gets put into my books. My friend, when I told her about the dream, was like, "We need to get you out, Sarah. You need to be dreaming about Zack Efferon, not Jack Nicholson." She's right. But no going out for me. I've got Sophia's book to write. More on that later.

So some of you know how this whole Liv series came about. Michael and I were on vid comm and he was like, "You should write a series about a blonde girl in LA who is sassy and short." I was like, "That's me." And MA was a genius because it worked. And here we are 12 books later. I couldn't give Liv a daughter, but I gave her a younger sister. My Lydia became Sophia, who she named. And incidentally, we've made great friends with someone who has a Liv and Sophia as daughters. Can you believe it?

Anyway, I think that this series did so well because I didn't have to think about how Liv spoke. She spoke like me. She responded like me. She's braver. Cooler. More bad ass. But she's really just me at the end of the day. And Sophia, well that's a lot of me too because Lydia is part of me. But different. I'm starting her series tomorrow and I'm so excited. And nervous. And grateful. Thanks for reading.

So back to Michael being an Amish. We were doing the cover for this book and Michael threw back the first attempt by our wonderful designer, saying that Liv was, "showing too much skin." Was she wearing a short skirt and a halter top? Oh no. Did she have on a thong bikini? Nope. Was she dressed like a stripper and wearing hooker shoes? No again. Liv was simply showing her bare arms.

*Gasp!* Oh, I know! I know!

I, of course, was like, "If it doesn't work for you, it doesn't work for you. We'll try something else." But secretly, in the back of my head, I was thinking, "Man, I'm going to tease the hell out of him for this." And so here we are. Our fearless leader, who has written so many different books with soldiers who go into battle with swords and guns blazing, cringes when he sees some naked arms. I know I called him Bird Killer in the last notes (although I love the review that said he should be Bird Assassin). I take back the name. We're calling him Amish Michael now.

And lastly, before I close us out. For those interested in the tunes that inspired the Liv series, here you go:

https://open.spotify.com/playlist/
3blVJMokv1MZsen23VyFgZ?
si=5yCKojSRQX2Mltvx2TJz4Q

Now, without further ado, I turn you over to Amish Michael, aka Bird Assassin, aka MA, aka Manderle, aka Please-Don't-Fire-Me-For-Teasing-You- Michael.

THANK You for reading this 12th and last book of the series, it has been a great ride!

So, I happen to find Sarah's personality (the part NOT directed at me) very funny. The whole Taco Bell becomes Organic Restaurant with Tacos is hilarious.

The "aka Please-Don't-Fire-Me-For-Teasing-You-Michael" I found funny, but a bit confusing.

Why would I fire her? I just got her settled into the right genre and having a great time in her life.

FOR EXAMPLE:

In the last two days, We have this going on behind the fiction...

The Setup: Sarah was asking about the next cover we need to do...

*Here are our texts:*

----------- START COPY -----------

sarahnoffke [1:18 PM]

Okay, any ideas on the cover that you want me to communicate with the artist? I'm wondering if the dragon should be bigger in the second cover? And positions?

michael [2:34 PM]

Dragon looking down, half a body (legs) sticking out of mouth, She is pointing up at him chastising him "YOU BETTER SPIT HIM OUT" ?

sarahnoffke [3:20 PM]

lol...no.

[3:21 PM]

Maybe dragon shooting fire right over your name? :wink:

[3:23 PM]

But I actually love the idea of the scene of her chastising him. He can mumble, "Spit what out?"

michael [10:22 PM]

"Spitth whath Outh?"

sarahnoffke [10:18 AM]

OMG. This totally has made me laugh out loud multiple times when I've thought about it.

michael [4:41 PM]

I'm telling you, it needs to be in the story!
It could become a long running joke.... "Where's Fido?"

"It wath only a smallth snackth"

sarahnoffke [6:27 PM]

Lol it's totally going in the book! I love it. Only twenty times today I've heard Lydia mumble, "Spppitt whath outh?"

And as of today, the dragon is trying to convince Sophia to <redacted>. "Life without <redacted> is meaningless."

michael [9:27 PM]

HAHAHAHAHAHAHA

----------- END COPY -----------

Yes, our typical daytime job conversations are every bit as odd as you might think.

## THE CONTINUING BEAUFONT FAMILY SHINANIGANS

Don't forget to either pre-order or buy (Read in Kindle Unlimited) (depending on when the book comes out) the S. Beaufont series...

You will appreciate the sheer awesomeness and size of the first 'book' as we are releasing book(s) 1 to 3 as the first volume.

BOOM SHAKALA!

The Uncommon Rider (The Exceptional S. Beaufont Book 1)

(We will see if Stephen Campbell changes my URL (we can't do affiliate links inside the book -found that out the hard way a few years ago.) Not sure what we do for links that take a reader to THEIR store.

<<Yes, Stephen Campbell changed the URL ;)>>

*Sarah Noffke – The Original Liv.*

# ACKNOWLEDGMENTS

## SARAH NOFFKE

My favorite part of writing any book is creating the acknowledgements page. It reminds me that writing a book is not a solo task. I might sit alone and write, but the finished product is a result of the support and encouragement of a tribe of people.

Thank you to the readers who buy the books, read them, review and recommend. YOU are the one who keeps us writing. I'm always inspired by the messages I receive from readers. Thank you supporting the books and offering so much richness to my life.

Thank you to my LBMPN family for all the support. Steve, Michael, Lynne, Moonchild, Jennifer and so many others who help champion the book to publication and beyond.

Thank you to the beta readers who offered so many valuable insights early on. Thank you to John, Chrisa, Kelly, Martin and Larry.

Thank you to the JIT team for all the awesome feedback. A new series is always exciting and nerve-wracking.

Michael and I thought we had a great idea for a new world, but we don't really know until we get objective feedback. What would I do without all you awesome readers?

Thank you to my friends and family. Writing is a strange profession. I work weird hours, talk to myself, have a strange diet, get antsy about deadlines. But the wonderful people in my life continue to show their encouragement and thoughtfulness no matter what. It is never lost on me because I know that I wouldn't be doing what I love without all you amazing people, cheering me on.

And as with all my books, the final thank you goes to my muse, Lydia. I wrote my first book so that I could make my daughter proud, and it's never stopped. I write every book for you, my love.

BOOKS BY SARAH NOFFKE

Sarah Noffke writes YA and NA science fiction, fantasy, paranormal and urban fantasy. In addition to being an author, she is a mother, podcaster and professor. Noffke holds a Masters of Management and teaches college business/writing courses. Most of her students have no idea that she toils away her hours crafting fictional characters. www.sarahnoffke.com

**Check out other work by Sarah author** here.

*Ghost Squadron:*

Formation #1:
**Kill the bad guys. Save the Galaxy. All in a hard day's work.**
After ten years of wandering the outer rim of the galaxy, Eddie Teach is a man without a purpose. He was one of the toughest pilots in the Federation, but now he's

just a regular guy, getting into bar fights and making a difference wherever he can. It's not the same as flying a ship and saving colonies, but it'll have to do.

That is, until General Lance Reynolds tracks Eddie down and offers him a job. There are bad people out there, plotting terrible things, killing innocent people, and destroying entire colonies. **Someone has to stop them.**

Eddie, along with the genetically-enhanced combat pilot Julianna Fregin and her trusty E.I. named Pip, must recruit a diverse team of specialists, both human and alien. They'll need to master their new Q-Ship, one of the most powerful strike ships ever constructed. And finally, they'll have to stop a faceless enemy so powerful, it threatens to destroy the entire Federation.

**All in a day's work, right?**

Experience this exciting military sci-fi saga and the latest addition to the expanded Kurtherian Gambit Universe. If you're a fan of Mass Effect, Firefly, or Star Wars, you'll love this riveting new space opera.

*NOTE: If cursing is a problem, then this might not be for you.*

*Check out the entire series* <u>here.</u>

### *The Precious Galaxy Series:*

*Corruption #1*
**A new evil lurks in the darkness.**
After an explosion, the crew of a battlecruiser mysteriously disappears.

Bailey and Lewis, complete strangers, find themselves

suddenly onboard the damaged ship. Lewis hasn't worked a case in years, not since the final one broke his spirit and his bank account. The last thing Bailey remembers is preparing to take down a fugitive on Onyx Station.

**Mysteries are harder to solve when there's no evidence left behind.**

Bailey and Lewis don't know how they got onboard *Ricky Bobby* or why. However, they quickly learn that whatever was responsible for the explosion and disappearance of the crew is still on the ship.

**Monsters are real and what this one can do changes everything.**

The new team bands together to discover what happened and how to fight the monster lurking in the bottom of the battlecruiser.

**Will they find the missing crew? Or will the monster end them all?**

*The Soul Stone Mage Series:*

House of Enchanted #1:

**The Kingdom of Virgo has lived in peace for thousands of years...until now.**

The humans from Terran have always been real assholes to the witches of Virgo. Now a silent war is brewing, and the timing couldn't be worse. Princess Azure will soon be crowned queen of the Kingdom of Virgo.

**In the Dark Forest a powerful potion-maker has been murdered.**

Charmsgood was the only wizard who could stop a

deadly virus plaguing Virgo. He also knew about the devastation the people from Terran had done to the forest.

**Azure must protect her people. Mend the Dark Forest. Create alliances with savage beasts. No biggie, right?**

*But on coronation day everything changes. Princess Azure isn't who she thought she was and that's a big freaking problem.*

**Welcome to The Revelations of Oriceran. Check out the entire series** here.

### *The Lucidites Series*:

Awoken, #1:
Around the world humans are hallucinating after sleepless nights.

In a sterile, underground institute the forecasters keep reporting the same events.

And in the backwoods of Texas, a sixteen-year-old girl is about to be caught up in a fierce, ethereal battle.

Meet Roya Stark. She drowns every night in her dreams, spends her hours reading classic literature to avoid her family's ridicule, and is prone to premonitions—which are becoming more frequent. And now her dreams are filled with strangers offering to reveal what she has always wanted to know: Who is she? That's the question that haunts her, and she's about to find out. But will Roya live to regret learning the truth?

Stunned, #2
Revived, #3

### *The Reverians Series*:

*Defects*, #1:

In the happy, clean community of Austin Valley, everything appears to be perfect. Seventeen-year-old Em Fuller, however, fears something is askew. Em is one of the new generation of Dream Travelers. For some reason, the gods have not seen fit to gift all of them with their expected special abilities. Em is a Defect—one of the unfortunate Dream Travelers not gifted with a psychic power. Desperate to do whatever it takes to earn her gift, she endures painful daily injections along with commands from her overbearing, loveless father. One of the few bright spots in her life is the return of a friend she had thought dead—but with his return comes the knowledge of a shocking, unforgivable truth. The society Em thought was protecting her has actually been betraying her, but she has no idea how to break away from its authority without hurting everyone she loves.

*Rebels*, #2

*Warriors*, #3

**Vagabond Circus Series:**

*Suspended*, #1:

When a stranger joins the cast of Vagabond Circus—a circus that is run by Dream Travelers and features real magic—mysterious events start happening. The once orderly grounds of the circus become riddled with hidden threats. And the ringmaster realizes not only are his circus and its magic at risk, but also his very life.

Vagabond Circus caters to the skeptics. Without skeptics, it would close its doors. This is because Vagabond

Circus runs for two reasons and only two reasons: first and foremost to provide the lost and lonely Dream Travelers a place to be illustrious. And secondly, to show the nonbelievers that there's still magic in the world. If they believe, then they care, and if they care, then they don't destroy. They stop the small abuse that day-by-day breaks down humanity's spirit. If Vagabond Circus makes one skeptic believe in magic, then they halt the cycle, just a little bit. They allow a little more love into this world. That's Dr. Dave Raydon's mission. And that's why this ringmaster recruits. That's why he directs. That's why he puts on a show that makes people question their beliefs. He wants the world to believe in magic once again.

*Paralyzed*, #2
*Released*, #3

**Ren Series:**

Ren: The Man Behind the Monster, #1:
Born with the power to control minds, hypnotize others, and read thoughts, Ren Lewis, is certain of one thing: God made a mistake. No one should be born with so much power. A monster awoke in him the same year he received his gifts. At ten years old. A prepubescent boy with the ability to control others might merely abuse his powers, but Ren allowed it to corrupt him. And since he can have and do anything he wants, Ren should be happy. However, his journey teaches him that harboring so much power doesn't bring happiness, it steals it. Once this realization sets in, Ren makes up his mind to do the one thing

that can bring his tortured soul some peace. He must kill the monster.

*Note* This book is NA and has strong language, violence and sexual references.

*Ren: God's Little Monster, #2*
*Ren: The Monster Inside the Monster, #3*
*Ren: The Monster's Adventure, #3.5*
*Ren: The Monster's Death*

## Olento Research Series:

*Alpha Wolf, #1:*
Twelve men went missing.

Six months later they awake from drug-induced stupors to find themselves locked in a lab.

And on the night of a new moon, eleven of those men, possessed by new—and inhuman—powers, break out of their prison and race through the streets of Los Angeles until they disappear one by one into the night.

Olento Research wants its experiments back. Its CEO, Mika Lenna, will tear every city apart until he has his werewolves imprisoned once again. He didn't undertake a huge risk just to lose his would-be assassins.

However, the Lucidite Institute's main mission is to save the world from injustices. Now, it's Adelaide's job to find these mutated men and protect them and society, and fast. Already around the nation, wolflike men are being spotted. Attacks on innocent women are happening. And then, Adelaide realizes what her next step must be: She has to find the alpha wolf first. Only once she's located him can she stop whoever is behind this experiment to create wild beasts out of human beings.

Lone Wolf, #2
Rabid Wolf, #3
Bad Wolf, #4